Thirteen Kinds of Love

Thirteen Kinds of Love

SOUMYA BHATTACHARYA

HarperCollins *Publishers* India

First published in India by
HarperCollins *Publishers* in 2019

Building 10, Tower A, 4th Floor, DLF Cyber City, Phase II,
Gurugram Haryana – 122002, India
www.harpercollins.co.in
2 4 6 8 10 9 7 5 3 1

A version of 'Something of Nothing' was first published in the *London Library* magazine.
A version of 'Pigeon Feathers' was first published in the *London Magazine*.

P-ISBN: 978-93-5357-276-1
E-ISBN: 978-93-5357-277-8

Typeset in 11.5/15.3 Cochin at
Manipal Digital Systems, Manipal

Printed and bound at
MicroPrints India, New Delhi

To Oishi
On turning eighteen

Every arrangement in life carried with it the
sadness, the sentimental shadow, of its not being
something else, but only itself

– Lorrie Moore, *Birds of America*

CONTENTS

PROLOGUE: IMPERIAL HEIGHTS

Late in the evening, I am struck by the different shapes of light. Standing on the road, looking up at Imperial Heights as it towers above me, I see globs of light – slivers, filaments, cylinders, rectangles and squares, I see points of light, bars of light, from beneath jambs of shut doors. A few curtains are drawn; some others have been thrown open to the night. On one curving balcony, fronting the floor-to-ceiling glass windows, I can faintly discern the figure of an elderly man who stands, hands gripping the railing, his shape indistinct in the gathered darkness, backlit by one of the living room lamps. Catching sight of a child playing the piano, I make up stories about what the music might be.

From those windows, particularly the ones in the apartments higher up, no sound drifts down on to the street. If two people are having an argument, to the onlooker they appear to be putting on a mime show. Only from the play area along the driveway, if it happens to be early evening, emerge the cries of children, the metronomic thump of a football being kicked back and forth, being slammed into a wall.

At the crest of a rise, alongside other towers with similarly self-important and far-fetched names (Palazzo Residency; Beverly Hill Heights; Tuscany), Imperial Heights stands – discreet, discrete.

Looking at the lights in those apartments or at the darkness in some, or at some curtains too heavy to be stirred by the light breeze, I wonder about the lives being lived there, their narratives continually unfolding.

I used to live in Imperial Heights. It was an eventful period in my life. And when I now come to this neighbourhood for some reason or the other, I still visit this lane sometimes, looking at the building, looking back on that phase of my life.

I look up at the tower and wonder about the people who inhabit it.

SOMETHING OF NOTHING

Rakesh winced as the car lurched over a pothole. A tremor of annoyance radiated through his hand that rested on the steering wheel. He had taken his eyes off the road again. Again, he had been looking at the mannequin in the Benetton shop window. It reminded him of Madam.

For months, he had wanted to step inside that shop. He would, for the first time, later today. Madam had asked him to collect a pair of jeans – *her* jeans! – that she had sent to be altered. He checked his reflection in the rear-view mirror. He was swarthy, clean-shaven, not unattractive, his skin stretched taut over a strong jaw. If he narrowed his eyes and knitted his brows, he could manage a look of brooding machismo even. When he looked at his own face, Rakesh quite liked what he saw.

His hair, gelled into a quiff early in the morning, was not holding up to the desired degree of rigidity. Rakesh noticed this in the mirror and swore. He raised and patted and mussed his hair till he was satisfied. As he righted his hair, his biceps – the impressive result of a lot of unremitting work – tensed. The short sleeve of his close-fitting T-shirt rode up. Rakesh smiled to himself.

He had first turned up at the Chaudhuris' home ten months ago, after someone who knew someone he knew had tipped him off that Mr Samrat Chaudhuri was looking for a driver. 'Arre, the family is good,' his acquaintance had told Rakesh. The smoke from the open fire over which dinner was being cooked on the pavement stung their eyes. On the filthy beach in front, fishing nets lay in a jumble of confused cobwebs. 'Look, Rakesh, you have no experience. To train, you need a job like the one they are offering. School, office, home. Nothing else.' He had winked and patted Rakesh on the back. 'See if you get lucky.'

Rakesh had rung the bell at 12A, the Chaudhuris' flat in Imperial Heights, one morning in the middle of a rainy spell. The rain had not let up in the past three days. Under a cloud-bloated sky, colour seemed to have leached from the city; trees and buildings had lost their definitions. It seemed hard to remember what everything looked like when it hadn't rained.

It was a Saturday. Samrat, his thin hairless legs protruding from his shorts and at odds with his flabby upper body, had opened the door, a beer in his hand. Learning that Rakesh was the driver who had come looking for a job, he had called out, 'Malini, that fellow has come,' and shuffled off down the hallway, leaving the door a little ajar. His voice had been friendly. Rakesh had been touched that Samrat had not shut the door in his face. Through the chink he had been able to catch bits of blonde wood cabinets, swirls of colours from paintings on the wall and, in a photograph, the face of a child with floppy hair.

Mrs Malini Chaudhuri had then emerged from one of the bedrooms, calling out to the maid to put the rice on to boil. She was shaking her hair dry. Standing at the entrance to the apartment, Rakesh had watched as beads of water had scattered and flown from her hair and, somehow managing to gleam even in that nothing-light, landed at her feet. His trousers, dripping, were rolled up to his knees. He held his umbrella in his left hand, fearful that it would muck up the marble floor if he put it down. He had glanced, guiltily, at the spreading puddle at his feet. In those days, his hair used to be parted on the left and combed across his head.

It had been settled in a few minutes. Rakesh had admitted that he had no real experience (at the Bombay port, he drove imported cars that had arrived from the gangway to a shed a couple of hundred metres away) and had agreed to a salary of ten thousand rupees. He had promised to be careful with the car and to always be polite. He had started work the following day.

Samrat was a senior executive in the creative side of an advertising firm. He spoke to Rakesh mostly in abstracted grunts and single words that indicated the destination he wanted to be driven to ('Worli', 'Parel', 'Juhu'), as though the effort of speaking in complete sentences was too monumental an undertaking. All the way to and from his office in Colaba at Bombay's southernmost tip, he worked on his laptop. Unlike his colleagues, Samrat did not go to parties. His only indulgences seemed to be reading or listening to music on his iPod, something that Rakesh had first mistaken for a fancy mobile phone. 'Sir, your phone,' he had called out, running after Samrat one day when he had left his iPod behind in the car, his arms outstretched as if he were holding out a votive offering, no more than the merest tips of his thumb and index fingers on the gadget. Samrat had taken it from him and smiled, a smile made up in equal parts of thanks, amusement, indulgence and almost imperceptible pity.

As he got to know him, Rakesh began to grow fond of the Chaudhuris' little boy, Arnab, making sure that he was never late to drive him to school. He was always vigilant in traffic when the boy was squirming around in the back seat with his mother. He carried Arnab's heavy school bag for him and enjoyed having him hang on to his finger when they crossed the busy road in front of the school gate. He took care of the boy's pet poodle when the family went on holiday. He offered Arnab a single rose, a red ribbon around its de-thorned stem, on his birthday.

And Malini? He dared not explain or attempt to articulate – even to himself, especially to himself – how she affected him. Malini was the one who made all the decisions that Rakesh thought important; it was she who steered the course of his – and her family's – day. She had come to trust Rakesh, often asking him these days about how they should do things. 'Shall we go to the petrol pump now or on our way back?' 'Do you think we might be better off going via Tulsi Pipe Road?' And she had started increasingly to adhere to his advice.

There were nights when Rakesh would lie on his thin mattress on the floor of his eight-foot-by-ten-foot room, very drunk on pay day, the edges of things blurring – the small stove at the foot of his bed spinning, with him in orbit around it. These were the times when he had visions of Malini – visions of her as she might have been in the bathroom, before she had attired herself and come to meet him on that first day, shaking the water from her hair.

Rakesh could never tell whether he had willed these visions into existence or whether they had appeared to him unbidden in a drunken stupor. He held them to himself and banished them, with equal ferocity. He felt as guilty as he felt envious; as ashamed of himself as he felt bold. The following morning, his head clear after he had rinsed himself under the thin rope of water from the communal tap at the corner of the road, he would have no recollection of the visions of the night before. There remained only an unidentifiable sense of unease.

Four months after he was hired, drivers at the office told him that he was getting ripped off and that they would find him a better-paying job, now that he had learnt to drive well. They insisted he ask the Chaudhuris for a raise.

Sleepless, Rakesh thought about it for two nights. More money was a great temptation. For starters, he could buy the pair of jeans he had been eyeing at a pavement stall on Linking Road. But what if the Chaudhuris refused? What if they thought he was too greedy and ungrateful and said they wanted to get rid of him? Would he find another job? Was it as certain as the drivers in the office said it was? Or were they simply leading him on?

Finally, having seen one of the drivers wearing a pair of jeans nearly identical to the one he wished to have, he realized that he would never be able to buy a pair like that if he didn't have more money. He wouldn't be able to get hair gel, which he now craved. In the three months at the Chaudhuris', he had begun to notice things he hadn't before; he had begun to covet them too. He wanted new clothes and a mobile phone with a large screen to watch music videos on. He pined for T-shirts that at least looked like the ones Samrat wore.

One evening, as he was giving her back the car keys at the end of the day's work, Rakesh asked Malini if his salary could be raised by another two thousand rupees. 'Of course, of course,' she said without a blink. The little boy hugged her knees. 'We were thinking of it in any case. You have come along well. We'll do it right away.'

As he walked home that evening, he paused to look at the big stores on Linking Road: Lacoste, Tommy Hilfiger, Esprit, Mango. He dared not walk in. They sold the same sort of clothes as the pavement stalls nearby did. But these stores seemed to enclose and epitomize a world utterly removed from the one the stalls stood for. How could the same thing, well almost the same thing, such as, say, a T-shirt, command such different prices and respect? He wanted to see what those items were like, to run his fingers under the collar of one of those T-shirts, caress the instep of one of those pairs of shoes.

Rakesh was thrilled that his salary had been raised by the exact amount that he'd wanted. At the same time, he felt angry and bitter because the amount meant nothing to the Chaudhuris. It was not even worth a moment's consideration before Malini had said yes.

'Yaar, the rich have their own problems,' one of the drivers at the office told Rakesh. 'We have nothing. We have nothing to lose.'

Rakesh did not resent the Chaudhuris' affluence, like their sudden trips to the five-star hotels near the airport or to the city's downtown. He did not mind Madam's frequent forays to *those* stores (especially the Benetton one) and her emergence from them, laden with huge, bursting paper bags, progressing towards the car like a stately ship towards its harbour, her purchases like billowing sails, her face still distracted from the present moment by the concentration she had needed to buy all that stuff in the store.

The Chaudhuris were good people, Rakesh believed. He was grateful to them. They had given him a job when no one else would have. They had given him a raise as soon as he had asked for one. They were unfailingly civil. They had bought him medicines that time he had fallen ill and paid for his visit to the doctor.

And yet, sometimes, when Madam and Sir bickered in low, taut voices that carried over to him in the hermetically sealed, air-conditioned, upholstered pod of the car, he wanted to turn around and scream: 'Don't you know how lucky you are?'

In the heat of an afternoon undisturbed by even the suggestion of a breeze, Rakesh manoeuvred the car into the lane alongside the Benetton showroom. He had on his favourite pair of jeans – mossy blue-green with an orange serpent coiling its way up from his knee to his thigh. His floral-patterned shirt was not tucked in – just as Shah Rukh Khan's in the movie *Don*. But during the brief walk from the car to the store, the shirt had begun to exhibit spreading damp patches under his arms and on his chest. Rakesh wiped his face with a handkerchief and then shoved his hand under his shirt and dabbed at his perspiring chest and armpits. Curious, anxious, afraid and confident, he stepped into the store, the chilly environs of which no summer could touch.

He had the piece of paper that he would have to hand over at the counter to get back Madam's pair of jeans. He kept it in his hand in case someone asked him why he was here. But no one did. People did not look at him. The ground floor housed the women's section and Rakesh saw – all for the first time, all at one go, all too much for him – women emerging from the changing rooms, pirouetting in dresses that had no proper sleeves, in dresses that were not much bigger than his handkerchief. He had involuntarily squeezed the paper in his hand into a tight ball. Uncrumpling it, he took the spiral stairway to the first floor, the men's department.

Standing there, amid the pressed, folded, hung glut of shirts, T-shirts, jackets, trousers and jeans, Rakesh's head began to swim. There was a pleasant and unfamiliar smell around him; he wondered where that up-tempo music was coming from.

He reached out and picked up a white T-shirt.

'Sir?' An attendant was immediately beside him.

'Can I try this on?' Rakesh asked in Hindi.

The attendant shrugged, unsmiling and pointed towards the changing rooms. Choosing one of the rooms, Rakesh slipped the T-shirt on, raised its collar, lowered it and examined himself from several angles in the full-length mirror. Peeling it off, he looked at the price tag: three thousand five hundred rupees, more than a quarter of what he made in a month.

He hurried downstairs, handed the paper over at the counter, cradled the wrapped package containing Madam's jeans as one would an infant and walked out.

Linking Road was empty, the pavement stalls dulled into a torpor by the heat. Rakesh swung the car around, spinning the steering wheel with unwarranted force. From the lane in which he had parked, he bulleted on to the main road and turned left towards his employers' home.

Through the windshield blazing with the afternoon light, he saw the cat – mottled grey-brown and not very large – begin its scamper-slink across the road. A cat crossing your path was a bad omen. All drivers waited for the cat to cross and then waited some more for the residue of that feline-induced bad luck to pass before driving on.

Rakesh revved his engine. He wouldn't let the cat get away. The cat's tail tensed, but it didn't look up. It scurried, but was bang in the middle of Rakesh's path as he closed in on it.

Rakesh hit the brakes with just a few feet between them. The cat darted across, still not looking up. A car was honking behind him.

'Next time, the next time you cross my path, chutiya, see what I do,' Rakesh mumbled. Then he drove on.

THE WAVE

'Sir! Sir?'

The call seemed to come from behind him. Reclined in his five-euro-an-afternoon, striped sun lounger with his book open in front of him, he turned his head around, index finger marking the place where he had stopped reading, his eyes, through his Wayfarer shades, trying to figure out who was calling him.

'Sir! Massage, sir?'

Shailesh Patil turned his head back towards the Mediterranean sky. He extracted his finger from the book and returned to it. The woman was addressing not him, but the Slavic-looking man in a deck chair in the row behind his. Bald and bullheaded, he lay on his stomach, eyes closed, his back like a gigantic pink sausage turned towards the sun. She was offering him a Thai foot massage. The man did not stir.

Eighteen months after retiring as the CEO of Johnson & Johnson, Shailesh still instinctively turned around, almost before he could help himself, whenever he heard someone say 'sir'. He had been called that for the better part of three decades. Even now, with his working life definitively over, it seemed as though that was his name, as though when someone called out 'sir', he, rightfully, was always the person being addressed.

Shailesh settled back into the chair and looked up at the blue dome above. There was something about that blue, his wife Nandini used to say – something pure and solid and crystalline, that made her want to come back time and time again, just to sit on a lounger and look up at it and across at the water. She had never been one for swimming, Nandini. Her particular pleasure, especially in her late-fifties – towards the end of a life that ended too soon – was carrying off a swimsuit and straw hat that would be the fashion statement of the season. She had the sort of grace and elegance that stopped just this side of hauteur, with the style that could make people passing by stop and glance at her. Shailesh used to enjoy that every time they came to the Spanish Riviera.

But if you'd asked, he would not have been be able to say quite why they had enjoyed coming to Torremolinos so much. It wasn't one of the fancier places like Marbella; it wasn't anything special; or at least it wasn't any more or less special than any of the other lesser-known small towns on the Costa del Sol. The same strip of beach; the same kitschy fridge magnets and beach sets and sandals

in the shops that lined the steep path – sometimes shaded by the eaves of buildings and sometimes burning in the sun – winding down to the edge of the ocean from the main road; the same waterfront restaurants serving tapas (anchovies, Nandini loved anchovies in vinegar, and Shailesh felt that no one ate them either more delicately or with more evident relish); the same pure blue of the sky and the sea; perhaps, who knew, even the same topless women in sunglasses that were bigger than their G-strings.

Shailesh had thought about this in the months after Nandini had died. The cancer was detected too late, it was already at stage four. She had gone very soon, not having to suffer for too long, as she had kept saying, the torment of its gradual spread. Shailesh had thought about it at length and it seemed to him that they came here so often because this was the first place they had holidayed at after their son had left home for graduate school in Boston. In those initial months of living without him, being in touch with him on email and the occasional phone call from a different time zone, those months of reorienting themselves with the altered rhythm of their lives, the holiday in Torremolinos had held a special place. It had shown them how valuable each of them was to the other; it had taught them, once more, and more tellingly, the worth of one another's company and love. The place had become for them pleasurably familiar. It had, like marriages, a lot to do with the excitement of the known and the intimate – the intimately known.

How many times had they been here? Six, was it? Or seven? Shailesh had not come – he could not bear to – after Nandini had died. He had not gone anywhere, really, ever since Nandini had died. He was wary of treading again the ground that he had trod with her, doing on his own the things they had done together. At the same time, he was curious about whether visiting on his own a place that they had liked to think of as 'theirs' (just as there were restaurants and songs and films they had thought of as 'theirs' for a variety of shared reasons) would sharpen his memory of her.

This was his first trip to a place outside Bombay; he was still wary of calling it a holiday.

The woman, in regulation oversized shades, a long, full-sleeved purple T-shirt that came to well below her thighs, her walk loose-limbed, a suggestive swing in her buttocks as though she was on the ramp, walked past Shailesh. Her olive skin was smooth and spotless. She probably had an all-year tan. Full of the confidence born of youth and radiant beauty – and an awareness of both – she looked around the strip of beach, finally zeroing in on a place to sit. Then she unrolled her pink towel, put her bag on the sand and settled down – cross-legged, back upright – a couple of feet away from Shailesh.

She sat facing him. She wanted the sun on her face, so she raised it – her tanned, slender neck, arched, towards the sky, embracing the warmth, delighting in it. Shailesh could bear to have the sun only on his back; he had kept his T-shirt on; the skin of his bare back stung in the Mediterranean heat. This weather must make you feel at home, people said to him when he visited Europe. How could he make them realize that it did not? In Bombay, which was hotter and stickier, he was not in any way really exposed to the heat and mugginess: the air conditioner ran all the time at home, in the car, at the office; he lived in a kind of parallel, temperature-controlled, tending-towards-Arctic-if-he-felt-like-it world. Here, while taking the public transport or walking, the sun – elemental and raw – scorched him. There was no buffer between him and the heat.

On this beach, and on others in France and Italy, Nandini and Shailesh used to play a private game. When someone young and beautiful – and seemingly proud of being so – came and sat near them, they would try to guess whether she would go topless. Looking at this woman, Shailesh remembered that old game. Yes, this one will, Nandini. This one will. The thing about dark glasses was that while you could look at what or whom you wanted to look at – say, the woman in front of you – there was no way the woman could know that you were looking at her. It was just as true the other way about, of course. Shailesh could not tell whether the woman was observing him.

She uncrossed her long legs, spread them out in parallel lines in front of her, then crossed them at the ankles, the palms of her hands flat on either side of her. She put in hours in the gym; you could tell from her perfectly formed arms and shoulders, the taut flatness of her stomach. She rummaged in her bag for something she did not find. Then she grasped the edges of her T-shirt and, in one fluent movement, pulled it up and over her body. She jerked her head free from it and shook her hair right back in place. She placed the T-shirt, now a balled-up kitten, on the towel beside her. She was not wearing a bikini top underneath. She sat cross-legged again, worshipping the sun.

Shailesh had stopped reading. The woman took out her mobile phone. She smiled. Shailesh tried to imagine her clothed, wearing a summer frock and silhouetted against the fading light in an arched doorway with a stained-glass window above it and church bells ringing in the background. He tried to imagine her without her bikini bottom. He smiled back.

Now that he had retired, Shailesh appreciated more fully what his job had meant to him in the months following Nandini's death. He had returned to it within a week of her passing away. His staff did not know quite how to deal with him. More deference or heightened distance? Condolences or calm professionalism? What would he *want*? The truth was that Shailesh had not known himself. He had probably wanted all of those things and none of them. But in that period of silent, confused, protracted mourning, of trying to learn to live from moment to moment, *in* each moment, and finding each moment just as hard to live in as the other, his job was the one changeless thing in a world in which nothing was as he had known for thirty years. The routine of it, its occasional irritations and dullness – the dullness about which he used to so bitterly complain – were invaluable.

He felt – irrationally, he now realized – annoyed when people asked how he was getting on. He found it crass. He found it insensitive when they didn't.

His son and his daughter-in-law visited from Pennsylvania and spent a fortnight with him. Although he never said it (what was there to say?), he resented it when they tidied up Nandini's belongings, when they cooked with the utensils that she had touched nearly every day, when they adjusted the tall lamp in the living room and, because of the fractionally altered position, the light fell at a different angle. To Shailesh, the apartment seemed crowded with their presence. Although they were intelligent and unobtrusive, unfailingly kind and sensitive, it seemed to him that merely by being there, they were suffocating him, leaving him with not enough space to grieve and remember.

In those days of obsessive remembering, almost anything anyone did felt like a violation – a desecration of Nandini's memory, of memories he wanted to never let go. It was a kind of obsessive remembering, trying to recollect and reconstruct with vividness many of the things that he associated with her: a certain tilt of the head when she was amused, a certain gesture of the hand when she tried to remonstrate with him. But like an image seen from too close, the details would get blurred or distorted. And Shailesh would begin to feel terrified that he would forget, that he was already beginning to forget.

He had had to recalibrate his whole life; he had to rearrange it around that absent centre that was Nandini. *Was.* The job, in those corrosive days, had helped. But even there, he had had to learn to return to an empty home; no, that wasn't the thing, really; he had had to learn to return to a home that would be forever empty.

There were so many other things that he had to learn. He had to learn to recognize and live with that particular blurred, half-conscious moment on waking up – the moment when one is sort of awake and is not, not entirely – that flicker of a second between when the mind has not grasped that everything has changed, and then, the moment when the mind does. That awareness comes like a physical blow. He had known silence when he used to be on his own at home, Nandini expected to return in a few hours or, when away on a work trip, in a few days. But now he had had to learn how the nature of that silence was different from the silence that surrounded him in his apartment in the months after her death. Standing on the balcony after dinner, leaning on the handrail and staring out across tiny patches of sky through the thick cross-hatching of leaves in the rain tree to his side, he could spot the moon. Nothing of that particular sight had changed. He would come out again with a drink and stare fixedly at that small scrap of sky and think of how everything goes on just the same even when nothing at all had remained the same for him. He had to learn to not instinctively call Nandini from his mobile, inadvertently punching the speed dial key to tell her something inconsequential about his day, something that could wait, of course, but felt as though it should not.

You'll get used to it, a lot of people had said. That was fucking nonsense. You did not get *used* to it. You began to inhabit a new reality that you had to construct.

That was why he was now re-reading this particular book. It described his new reality so precisely. The young writer who had moved into the least imperial of all the apartments in Imperial Heights, had recommended the novel to Shailesh. It was by a neglected and nearly forgotten Bengali writer called Amitesh Bandopadhyay. It was about a man whose wife dies, leaving behind a young daughter, and how he deals with his loss.

Shailesh re-read the bit that seemed to him like a coda for the novel. 'There began after that a period when I was continually bewildered: Was the worst over or was it just about to strike? I never could tell.' That was just it. If he were to successfully construct a new life and be able to carry on with it, this was the question Shailesh would have to first find an answer to.

The woman got up. She tested how hot the sand was with the tips of her toes. Kicking the sand up a bit, she let it trickle down between her toes and fall at her feet. Still facing Shailesh, she raised her arms. He followed the lift of her breasts and then the manner in which they settled down as she lowered her arms by her sides. With her thumb and index fingers, she kneaded her neck and shoulders. She moved her neck methodically and rhythmically from side to side, ten turns this way and then the other – the sort of exercise a physiotherapist might recommend as a palliative for the travails of sitting at a computer for hours every day.

She then turned around and walked into the sea. She treaded the water and then went further in, letting the ocean lap against her thighs. Sprinkling water over her breasts, her stomach, her shoulders and her arms, she turned around again to face the sun.

Shailesh stood up, arched his back and stretched. He touched his toes. He was still lanky, the shock of white hair pulled back from the high forehead was still abundant, but he had acquired a stoop in the past year.

Soon, the woman was returning to her place on the sand. Looking at her now, alone on this stretch of intimately known beach, was different from looking at many such women during his holidays here with Nandini. In those days, this sort of thing had seemed like a joke, a sort of surreptitious game played between themselves.

Now? He simply couldn't tell. The past is a foreign country. But how differently did one do things in the present?

Shailesh had nearly drowned here once. He was a sturdy swimmer and not a little vain about how far in he could go when men younger and fitter than him would prance around three feet into the water. On this occasion, he had not actually gone very far into the sea. But something – he was still not quite sure what – had happened. Had he been caught in a whirlpool? A riptide? So, there he was – certainly not as far out as he would usually go – trying to ride the waves to return, when it struck him that the waves were not throwing him towards the shore. Or not throwing him as far forward as he would have liked. He crested a wave and was flung forward, but before he could gain his balance, he was sucked back again. Bit by bit. One step forward and two or even three back.

Once panic began to engulf him (the strong tow in the water when he was being pulled back – a tow that he could not combat, however hard he tried), he began to wave at the shore. Not waving but drowning. Nandini, in her inevitable straw hat, waved back. Spitting out water, his lungs feeling torn with the effort of clawing his way towards the beach, to not yield to the furious current that kept dragging him away, he thought he could see her smile. After that, confident in his prowess as a swimmer, she had returned to her book. Not once did she look up.

Panting and coughing, he had then started shrieking for help. But it was windy, he had no power in his lungs and the waves were noisy around him. His cries did not travel. In the end, two men joshing each other a little distance away had happened to glance at him. They had noticed the terror in his eyes, his foam-flecked mouth. They had come towards him and, standing a little distance away (perhaps to stay out of reach of the whirlpool in which he may have been), had taken hold of him. Each had grasped one of his arms and together they had dragged him to the shore. There Shailesh had collapsed, exhausted, still frightened, for once facing the sun as he had taken laborious breaths lying on his back.

He had never told Nandini this. Until she was dying. That was when he felt, he knew not why, that it would be some sort of transgression to hide this from her for ever. He told her in the hospital, during her last stay there before she died. Frail and tired, she was slipping in and out of consciousness. He did not know what she heard, whether she comprehended anything at all. When he was done, his face close to her ear, the fingers of his right hand entwined with those of her left, she had nodded. 'It's all right, it's all right,' she had said, patting his cheek with her right hand.

The woman sat down again. Her body was glistening with droplets of water. She did not towel herself; the sun would soon dry her out. She took out her mobile phone again and sent what seemed like a long message.

Shailesh knew all about love and desire and the desire that was engendered by love. Or at least he thought he knew enough about it, as much about it as he wanted to. But what about unmitigated desire without love at its centre? Unmitigated desire that had nothing to do with love? How, with the one thing divorced from the other, do you deal with it? The lessons he had learnt about this matter in his youth, at university in England

and while working in that country, long before Nandini, long before desire with love at its heart took over his life – those lessons were of no use to him now. He could remember them only dimly; he might as well have not tried because the circumstances had changed. And that altered everything.

She smiled again. Shailesh looked her in the eye. Should he take off his sunglasses? Then she waved. Shailesh raised his arm to wave back.

Then he saw the shadow alongside him.

The man, lean and of medium height, his hair fashioned into spikes that stood up with a gelled gleam, strode past him towards the woman. He was wearing a round-necked T-shirt and shorts, and he had a beach bag slung over his shoulder. From his right hand dangled a blue-and-white icebox, the kind of thing, packed with beers, you take for a long day on the beach.

He reached the woman and bent down. She, still sitting, reached up and wrapped her arms around his neck.

They kissed.

MOBILE ATTACK

Some weeks ago, Ajit Dandekar's son had asked him: 'Dad, do you feel awful when you have to let yourself into the flat and it's dark and you have to switch the lights on yourself?' Ajit pretended to study the label on a bottle of diet mayonnaise. 'Hmm. Mmm?' He knew what Sachin wanted to hear. He knew that he would have to be careful about how he phrased his reply.

'Dad, do you feel awful if you have to let yourself into the flat and it's dark and you have to switch the lights on yourself?' the seven-year-old asked again, his tone ascending in pitch, insistence braided into the question mark at the end of the sentence.

'Well, I used to live on my own for years, Sach. So I don't particularly mind. But all that was before you were born. Now it feels odd when I come home and you aren't here. But that doesn't happen very often, does it? Yeah,

I would much rather have you at home when I return. It makes me happy.'

'That's not a proper answer, Dad.'

No, it wasn't, and Ajit knew. He had disappointed his boy. But he hadn't been able to come up with a more unequivocal way of framing his response. The answer actually was yes and no; but it would have been disastrous to have said so. More often than not, Ajit came home before his wife. The boy was on his own till then. Of course Ajit loved to have his son fling himself at him as soon as he opened the front door. Of course he loved the lights on, the books strewn on the table, the smell of food from the kitchen, and the anecdotes from his day at school.

But sometimes, just sometimes, he liked the quiet order and stillness of returning to an empty apartment; the sense of control and space that the uninhabited state of the apartment afforded; the amplified sound of the switches being flicked on, the light swallowing the incumbent darkness, the freedom to sit where he liked for a few moments in silence, to kick off his shoes and put them back in the closet after a while, to fling his clothes on to the bed and watch TV with the volume turned right up. (You don't do those things when your little son is around; setting a good example becomes a cornerstone of the responsible father's life.)

Ajit's wife, Priyanka, worked in the human resources department of a large conglomerate. She kept inhuman hours. Her colleagues called her at any time they felt they needed her help, at any time at all they wanted things sorted out. On occasion, they would call Priyanka from New York or Los Angeles (cities the senior staff of the company frequently visited) when it was afternoon in the US. It would be well past midnight in Bombay by then. Priyanka never switched off her mobile phone; her job was such that she could never even afford to turn it silent.

Ajit wondered how she managed. But she managed all right, instilling a sense of calm and order at home, distilled from the chaos of the workplace. She had texted him this afternoon, saying that he needn't bother, she had nipped out at lunchtime and bought the ball of wool, felt-tipped pens and whatever else – he couldn't even remember, now – that Sachin needed for a project in school. 'Without you …' he had texted her back. No, Ajit would never be able to do without Priyanka. He would never be able to do what Priyanka did for the family. He got too wound up about things at work, felt too much on edge, too annoyed too often; and the frustration born of anger often got the better of him.

On days when that happened, Ajit didn't mind – no, he actually enjoyed – returning to a dark and empty flat. On days such as today. It had been dreadful in the office. He didn't want to think of it or tell his wife about it. Without Priyanka and Sachin around, he would be able to collect himself and put the rancour of the day behind him. At least for tonight. He would tell her about it tomorrow evening, perhaps. They would not be able to laugh about it (he was never able to laugh about these things), but at least he would be up to talking about it. For the moment, Ajit wanted to not have to talk any more, to not talk to anyone for a while. He wanted to sit in his leather armchair, in front of the 64-inch TV and have a quiet drink or two. Or three. Or four.

Priyanka worried about what Ajit had to deal with at his office, the hostility that he often had to face. She had made him – essentially a sedentary man with a fondness for sweets and red meat – join a gym a year ago. Ajit had taken surprisingly well to the regime of daily cardio and light, and then heavy, weights. And once his fat began to burn away, the contours of his muscles began to get pronounced, he delighted in wearing T-shirts that were a size too small for him; for the first time in the eleven years that they had been married, Priyanka saw him unselfconsciously emerge from the shower with only a towel draped around his waist. Priyanka encouraged what had now become her husband's gym addiction. At the same time, she could not keep herself from worrying. You couldn't be too careful. Forty-one was a risky age. And there was nothing one could do about the stress he encountered and the manner in which he responded to it. She knew, she was in HR. Only last year, a perfectly healthy colleague …

Say what you will about their jobs, but between them, the money was generous. It paid for their lavish annual holidays abroad; the fees of the elite private school to which Sachin went; the tennis lessons; the black Audi, the silver Toyota and the two drivers; and their home in Imperial Heights in Bandra, constructed by knocking down the wall between the flats 9A and 9B. Now known as merely 9B, this flat had four bedrooms, a 600-square-foot living room ... Ajit loved having acquaintances over so he could show them where he lived, and how. It defined him in a way little else did.

But on a day such as today, he found that the manifestations of his hard-earned affluence did not make up for the ordeals that his job inflicted on him at times. Ajit was a marketer, the vice president of marketing in one of the country's largest newspapers. And he could not bear the editors with whom he had to work to promote and market what he called the product and they – with dour insistence – called the paper. They were contemptuous of the way he spoke and wrote emails ('Did they teach you about split infinitives in management school?'). They were dismissive when he suggested ideas for what could be done in the paper. And they lost no opportunity to let him know that, to them, he and all the marketing guys in his department were interlopers, mere fickle professionals who could be marketing a newspaper today and detergent tomorrow. The suggestion of course, was that they – the journalists – were unsullied by such promiscuousness and were devoted to only the media.

How did they get away with it? In Ajit's previous job with a mobile phone company, no one would have stood for this kind of nonsense. At least no journalist could imagine living in Imperial Heights, not even in an apartment half the size of theirs.

Ajit noticed that he had flung his shoes right across the floor. He drank the first Laphroaig neat, relishing the burn that travelled down his throat and stomach. In the lift, on his way up, he had met Shailesh Patil from 6B, the former CEO of Johnson and Johnson, recently widowed, even more recently retired, his demeanour marked by mild bafflement now that his CEO days were over. 'No supply of water tomorrow,' he had informed Ajit with solemn authority. 'Better be prepared.'

He had better phone the guys who brought those water tankers. He reached for his smartphone. He touched a key; the screen refused to offer its luminous, familiar glow. Was the bloody thing on the blink? He pressed and pressed again, then he took out the battery, slid out the SIM card and blew on the damn thing as Sachin – much more at ease with these things than he was – had once taught him, and then he put it all back in. The screen remained obdurately dark. Not a flicker of life. Fuck it. He would wait for Priyanka to come back and call them. At least the bastards at the office would not be able to reach him.

The little shits. Supercilious and pompous. He could do their jobs, but they not his. He had been to the Indian Institute of Management, not they. What did they do apart from being patronizing and affecting faintly bohemian airs? He especially resented the editor, his lower lip turned downward in perennial contempt, his thin smile always holding in it a hint of a sneer, the man who could barely say hello without freighting the greeting with a sense of ironic malice. The editor thought of himself as The Editor. Just as most editors did. Just as his predecessor had.

Earlier this year, they had been to a conference together about how the media was changing and what news organizations ought to do to keep up with the changes – change from being newspapers to 24/7, multi-platform delivery outlets for content. All the talks were given by American media professionals who, having seen a host of their own papers close down one by one, were making a living by telling media executives in India – a country in which newspaper sales were still rising – how to run their companies.

One of the speakers told them how the editorial and marketing departments in American newspapers had always been at odds with each other. 'Then American editors realized something: Marketing is too important to be left in the hands of the marketing department. It was imperative for journalists and marketers to work together.' The Editor, who had been sitting, sullen and slack-jawed with his colleagues at the back of the conference hall, probably feeling insulted by the fact that the journalists and marketing guys had to participate in the same seminar, cackled and hooted. Ever since, at every argument, he had been repeating this line. The fucker.

Anyway, perhaps The Editor would be fired. Like his predecessor, with whom Ajit had had a bitter, uncivilized verbal brawl the morning after the terror attacks in Bombay. (Looking back now, he ought not call it a 'verbal brawl'; it was just that the other man had been uncivilized and Ajit had been bitter about it afterwards.) That morning, the headline across the front page was 'BLOODIED'. 'What sort of a headline is that? What does it *mean*? I can't quite ...' Ajit – harried, baffled, disappointed, other newspapers rolled up in his hand, like some sort of weapon – had asked. The Editor (well, he was now no longer The Editor – serves him right, he was now The-One-Who-Used-To-Be Editor, as far as Ajit was concerned), looking more dishevelled than usual, his eyes bloodshot, his greying hair sticking up at angles from his head, drumming a pencil on the table and his eyes on the TV in front of his desk, had, without even looking at him, said, 'What kind of a fucking question is that? Do they teach you to be especially stupid in management school?' That same phrase. Management school. As though going to management school and then working for a newspaper was some irredeemable sin. It got ugly. The Editor had screamed, 'On a day like this I don't have the patience to have a conversation with a fucking neo-literate like you.'

Six months later, he was gone. The paper's coverage of the attacks had been found to be inadequate. Perhaps Ajit had been right; perhaps that headline had started it all and he had, even at that time, seen it for what it had been: stupid. The rival newspapers had done much better. Covering the biggest news story in India in the decade, their paper's readership had fallen, while those of its competitors had gone up.

That Editor had got the boot. And Ajit? Well, here he was: senior general manager at the time of the terror attacks, vice president within a year and a half. The second Laphroaig tasted better; it was mellower, there was not as much burn. The little shits.

No, he couldn't bear to think of his run-in with The Editor today.

Chelsea was playing Spurs at Stamford Bridge. Ajit switched the TV on. He turned the volume up as high as it would go. The six giant Bose speakers transformed the living room into a mini stadium. The Editor supported Arsenal. He said that Chelsea was a plutocratic club run by a Russian oligarch and his dirty money. He had told Ajit this in the only conversation they had had – why? Why had they had it anyway? – about football. Of course he would support Arsenal. He couldn't appreciate the Chelsea players for who or what they were. He couldn't admire Lampard and Terry and Kante and Costa and Hazard. Instead he had to use some dumbass ideology and philosophy and god knows what other crap as the rationale for not supporting one of the best club football teams in the world. Chelsea had won the Premier League far more often than Arsenal had in the recent past. Chelsea had won the Champions League, for fuck's sake. Ajit didn't mind plutocrats.

Hah, Arsenal. Not won the league since 2004. The Editor *would* support them, wouldn't he? Fucking loser. Fucking losers.

Laphroaig number three wasn't making him any more mellow. On the contrary, the blackness of his mood was returning, like swiftly falling darkness at the end of a febrile day. The whisky was heightening his animosity and impotent anger. He was talking to himself, aloud. Resentment was unleashing incensed sentences, which invited more incensed sentences and they entwined themselves inside his head before being uttered aloud, coherent. They roiled about in the air around him, polluting the atmosphere of the living room that was alive with the dramatic voices of excitable football commentators.

The vein in Ajit's temple was beginning to throb. He reached for his phone again. On the phone's dark screen, he jabbed, this time with unwarranted violence, at where the keys should have been. The phone refused to come to life. What were Priyanka and Sachin doing at the bloody birthday party? He felt a heaviness in his body. He felt unwilling to get up. Hazard had scored. Chelsea was a goal up. At least that was something. How on earth could he reach Priyanka?

With a vague sense of reproach, Ajit looked at the spot where the landline telephone used to be. It had never had a proper table. Just for effect, it would be propped up on the empty tin case of a bottle of Bowmore. Ajit had made Priyanka get rid of the thing six months ago.

'You have two mobile phones, Priyanka. I have one. God knows that in a few years, once he starts going to tuitions on his own, we'll have to get one for Sachin. Why do we need a landline?' Ajit had said one evening, reopening his flank of attack in a well-worn disagreement.

'It's good to have it,' Priyanka said. 'Security. It being there doesn't harm us, does it?'

'Well, we pay the bills for it, don't we? A rental of five hundred rupees every month for nothing. When did you last make a call from it?'

'Oh, come on, Ajit, don't be silly. Since when did five hundred rupees become so unaffordable?'

'No, it's just the principle of it. And the bloody nuisance. It conks out nearly every month. We complain to the telephone office. They take a week to fix it. And then it conks out again. It's not just the money, you are right. But why should we waste all that effort to have something we genuinely don't need?'

'Don't be stubborn,' Priyanka had said. The firmness in her tone was inlaid with weariness. They had gone down this road too many times – and, as far as she could see, for no reason. It wasn't worth the trouble.

'Don't be stubborn, Priyanka. Whoever uses a landline these days? It's so twentieth century. Even our grocer uses only a mobile phone. India has more mobile phones than the population of America. And the damn thing *looks* ugly sitting there. I can't bear the sight of it.'

'Okay, can we simply stop talking about this for now?'

They did. And that was the last argument they ever had about the landline. The next time the service to the phone was disrupted, Ajit got his way. One Sunday morning, picking up the receiver and holding it to his ear on an impulse (they really did hardly ever use it) and finding the phone dead, Ajit said, 'All right, this goes in the trash. Now.' Priyanka, who was ordering a takeaway lunch from one of her mobile phones, did not even look up.

It suddenly struck him how, along with landlines, the phone book – with numbers painstakingly written by hand – had become obsolete. Everyone had all the phone numbers they needed in the address books of their phones. No one actually remembered phone numbers any longer; they simply called them up from their mobile phones. Ajit did not bother dropping the clunky instrument into a cardboard box. He carried it, arms swinging, down the stairs (it's good to do stairs, avoid the lift when you can), took it to the trash can in the apartment block's rear courtyard and dropped the phone into it with a clatter. There. Done. Reuse. Recycle. If you can.

As the sweat, as if almost out of nowhere, began to bead his brow in the air-conditioned room, Ajit felt that he had been wrong in the matter of the landline and Priyanka had been right. Security, she had said. He knew her number by heart, he knew he knew, but he seemed to have trouble remembering it. But if he tried, if he tried hard to focus, would he be able to? But then, how would he call? How could he reach Priyanka? He shook the handset and hit the side of the chair with it. He wanted to kick it, then didn't. It was unwise; it also appeared to be too much of an effort.

The stabs of pain seemed to emanate from somewhere near his chest. Increasingly, they were becoming like jolts. And, no, not just his chest. They were taking possession of his whole body. He could barely sit in his chair. He could barely move from it. He was sheathed in sweat. His throat. He wanted water. He could not distinguish the words in the commentary. There was just a wall of sound. He was trapped inside a vortex of pain that was sucking him further and further in. He could not get up. The bloody phone. He fumbled with it.

Priyanka and Sachin let themselves in when no one opened the door after they had rung the bell. They found Ajit at an awkward angle in his favourite chair. His phone was on the floor.

Chelsea was three goals up.

PIGEON FEATHERS

At that time the boy had had no idea that this was the last thing they were doing as a family.

He was the one who had discovered the pigeon. It was plump and seemed canny. It sat immobile for hours in the pot behind the tall plant on the ledge of the kitchen window. Intermittently, it snapped its head from side to side as though alert to prying eyes or danger. 'Ma, Ma! Mamma!' he shrieked, taking care to let his breath out only when he was out of the kitchen. He ran full tilt across the living room where his father sat reading, and into his parents' bedroom.

Usually, on seeing something out of the ordinary, he would have first attracted his father's attention. But this was something out of the ordinary in the kitchen and that was his mother's domain; his father tended to feign ignorance about what happened inside the kitchen although he showed great keenness and occasional appreciation for what emerged from it. Besides, his father had seemed distracted and irritable for some days now. Must be the office.

Mrs Malini Chaudhuri turned away from the French windows that ran along the length of one of the bedroom walls. She had been looking at the bank of green visible from their twelfth-floor flat, the waxy iridescence imparted to the leaves by a spell of sunlight after a fierce shower. This view was one of the reasons why they had chosen to rent this flat so many years ago. They could barely afford it then. Now, the fact that they had been hard-pressed to rent it as well as the memory that she and her husband, in amicable intimacy, had together taken such a crucial decision, seemed impossibly distant, almost impossible. For years, the rent had no longer pinched. But they knew that, with a single income – however generous – they would not, like most of their neighbours, ever be able to buy this apartment. They were merely tenants; nonetheless, 12A, Imperial Heights had come to stand for the notion of a home of their own.

The weather was of the indecisive sort that couldn't make up its mind about whether to be sunny or cloudy. She inhaled the moistness in the air.

'Arnab, be careful, don't upset the vase. What it is it?'

The boy would not tell her. His hair flopping (Malini made a mental note about getting him a haircut), he dragged his mother to the kitchen and, silent, tense with expectation and excitement, he pointed at the pigeon.

The bird paid them no attention at all. It merely shifted slightly on the mound of soil beneath the plant, and remained snug, its back to the raised brown rim of the pot.

'She will lay eggs there, Arnab. Don't disturb her,' Malini said. The boy stifled a squeal, unable to quite believe that this drama was unfolding right in their kitchen. 'Take a photo with your phone, Mamma, take a photo. Right now.' He tumbled out of the kitchen and, did a fist pump in the hallway. 'Yay!' He skipped into the living room to tell his father.

When Samrat Chaudhuri ambled into the kitchen with Arnab tiptoeing in front of him, Malini was draining pasta at the sink. They held each other's gaze for a moment, but did not speak. 'Lunch will be ready at one,' said Malini, looking at the sieve. These days, especially in front of their son, they found it hard to look at each other when they spoke. It was as though they were both complicit in a betrayal: ashamed of the fact that things had come to this; disappointed that they had; and guilty that they had not yet been able to bring themselves to be forthright with the boy.

As Samrat and Arnab approached the window, the bird plumped up her feathers.

'Ah, we'll have eggs soon, Arnab. Would you like to eat the eggs?'

The boy looked up, bewildered. 'I want to see the chicks hatch!'

Samrat ruffled his son's hair. Arnab had grown taller over the past year. He now came up to Samrat's waist. He nuzzled his father's stomach. Samrat held him close, rather too tight and for rather too long. The boy had to extricate himself after a little while.

The eggs arrived two days later, on a Tuesday. Arnab rang his father up. Samrat was in the middle of a meeting with an important client who was of the opinion that the advertising creative for a new shampoo was too cluttered and the copy wasn't quite communicating how unique the product was. 'Excuse me, sorry,' he said, glad for the interruption. He stepped out of the conference room.

'Baba, the eggs are here. I saw them.'

'Why are you speaking in a whisper? I can barely hear you.'

'Because I don't want to scare her.'

'Can't you walk out on to the balcony?'

Silence. 'Yes, I am in the balcony now. I can't believe it. One of them is slightly brownish. In bits. There is something on it. I don't know what that is. The other one is pure white.'

Samrat smiled. 'Good. I'll see them when I am back home.'

'No, it will be too dark for you to see them then. That's why I am describing them to you.'

'Oh, thanks. I'll see them tomorrow, in that case.'

'Baba?'

'I've got to go. I'm sorry.'

'No, one moment, Baba ... When will the chicks come out?'

'You need to be patient. We may not get chicks. Let's see if we are lucky.'

'Why don't all eggs give chicks? Baba?'

'Look, I've got to go. Ask Mamma. Where is she?'

'On the other phone. Discussing homework with Paul's mum.'

'I see. All right, see you in the evening.' Samrat walked back to the charged atmosphere of the conference room. He could see Malini, her legs folded beneath her, a pen in hand, sitting close to the window, her hair catching the gleam of the afternoon sun, sorting out the homework.

From that afternoon, Arnab began to have his breakfast and lunch in the kitchen. He would eat standing up at the counter, next to the sink, elevated by a small stool to the height that was just right for him. As he ate, he looked at the pigeon, observing her every little movement, keeping an eye on the eggs when she adjusted her body.

On Friday, the first egg hatched. Arnab returned from school to see something tiny and brown on the soil. It was quite unlike a bird, in fact quite unlike the chicks he had seen in picture books when he was younger. It had no beak. You could hardly tell one part of its body from another. You could hardly tell that it had a body or even parts of it. Shells lay all around it and the fluffy thing was largely covered by its mother most of the time.

The second, identical chick he spotted after breakfast on Saturday. Arnab's mother began to complain that it was getting to be impossible to drag him out of the kitchen. He stopped playing with his friends downstairs; he offered to do his homework in the kitchen, in the manner in which he ate, standing on a stool beside the sink with his exercise book on the counter.

'We'll have to tell him. How long can we go on like this?' Malini said on Saturday night. She was dabbing, in precise, firm, circular motions, moisturizer – and a host of other unguents – on her face. She still looked about ten years younger than her thirty-six. Samrat gave her a look, a quick one, in the mirror.

'But he is so absorbed with those birds. Let's see what happens to them. Let that excitement subside a bit.'

'Yes, it would be a shame to hit him with this now.' Malini sighed.

Caring for these birds was the last thing they were doing as a family, they both knew. Were they glad that it had allowed them to put off announcing to Arnab the news of their impending separation? They had no idea if he had sensed anything. He was a bright child. But he had not let on. And they couldn't dare guess how he would take it.

Samrat and Malini now slept on either side of their king-sized bed, each towards one edge, curled up on their sides, their backs to each other, taking up as little space as possible. It seemed as though they were conscious, even while asleep, that they dare not face each other, far less even drift towards one another. They had bought separate blankets some weeks ago.

Sometimes, when, during the course of moving around in the flat, they inadvertently touched one another, they said sorry. They supposed that it would be different later, in the years to come when they would have reconciled themselves to the event; they imagined, both of them, that they would be friendly towards each other, that they would be mature and that they would both be there for Arnab. He mustn't suffer on account of their folly. Now, in the weeks of adjusting to a state that was a new actuality but still withheld from their son, that wasn't yet an official one and wasn't quite real, they floundered and were diffident with each other.

As they had had for years, they still had drinks and a home-cooked special dinner together on Saturday nights. They continued to uphold the custom as much for the sake of their son – who, if both his parents were at home, had never seen them deviate from this ritual – as from a sense of habit or even from a want of anything else to do. And on some of these occasions, after the coffee, one of them would unselfconsciously put his or her hand on the other – an unspoken code that meant no, I will wash the mugs, or no, I will put out the breakfast things for tomorrow. In those moments, Samrat and Malini felt as if they were together mourning the demise of something that was once more precious to them than anything else. Mourning, but from a sort of distance; grieving for something they had deliberately given up rights to grieve for any longer. Back in the bedroom, out of sight of their son, they would retreat to their separate sides of the bed. Once, they would cleave to each other. Now, they had been cleaved apart.

How had it come to this?

How did it? How does something come to be something else? Is it really possible to know when the thing itself is changing all the time?

Samrat and Malini had tried. They had tried to parse it, break it down, find reasons, find solutions. They had procrastinated, been in denial. And in the end, after so many years, and so many years of trying, they had to acknowledge it. There was no escape from it any longer. And it came down to three words: It wasn't working. Whatever 'it' was. There had been no obvious betrayal. Or at least no obvious betrayal concerning someone of the opposite gender. After the fights, after the negotiations, after the attempts to fix what was evidently broken, they had merely arrived at the end of something. Mutual incompatibility, the courts called it. Not a bad phrase. As vague as it was accurate. Why not, when one of the reasons one married was the vague and accurate hope of mutual compatibility?

But not even now, at this stage when they were as weary of what it had come to as wary of what lay ahead, could they explain either to themselves or to each other exactly *how* it had come to this.

Each of us remembers the same story in different ways.

The chicks were beginning to look like chicks. They had eyes now and small, pointed orange beaks. They had lost much of their down, but had not yet acquired plumage and they still did not resemble their mother. Arnab would sometimes spot them on their own during the afternoon, concealed behind the plant and notice the mother return towards the evening. He watched her feed them, transferring food to their beaks from her own. Often, there would be more food around them on the cold soil and all over the kitchen ledge than inside them. And the ledge and the plates and cups put out there to dry would be full of feathers they had shed.

'They are a real nuisance,' Malini said in exasperation one afternoon. 'This place stinks and it is filthy beyond belief. The maid has to wash all the utensils twice over.' She glared at Arnab, as though it was all somehow his fault. Arnab said nothing. He gave his mother a look made up in equal parts of bemusement and reproach.

He began to notice another pigeon paying them the occasional visit. 'That must be the father. He has begun to visit,' Arnab told Malini. 'Where was he all this while? Do you think the chicks miss their father? He comes only so seldom.'

He gave them names – Franny and Zooey – picked up from a book of Samrat's that was lying face down on the coffee table. He could tell one from the other. Franny was the swifter learner and the faster grower. It began to waddle around before Zooey could ('Looks like Shane Warne coming into bowl,' Samrat said to Arnab and they both laughed aloud at the joke). It started to flap its wings with energy and eagerness as Zooey looked on, silent and still.

'They will grow up and fly away soon, Arnab,' Malini said one night over dinner. She did not look at Samrat. She knew that he wouldn't look up from his plate. And she knew he knew why she had said that, how their departure would mean that they would no longer be able to postpone telling their son about their now-cleaved life – and his.

Rakesh, their driver, knew something was amiss in the household in which he now felt so much at home. Samrat, who would previously only grunt the names of places to which he wanted to be driven, had suddenly become loquacious, asking him about his father or when he next wanted to visit his mother in their Uttar Pradesh village or how the plans for his sister's wedding were coming along.

Malini, for so long the fulcrum around which his working day revolved, had turned withdrawn, taciturn. She seemed mostly distracted. In his rear-view mirror, Rakesh could see her looking out of the window and not patting her hair back after it had become windblown. She still went on shopping expeditions, but she rarely emerged, even if laden with those huge bags, with her face flushed with pleasure. No longer would she solicit his opinion on which route to take. Instead, rather like Samrat in the old days, she simply told him where she wished to go. Once, when Rakesh asked her if she preferred one route to the other, she said: 'Oh, it doesn't matter, let's just get there as quickly as we can.'

Zooey became infected with something towards the middle of the following week. They couldn't be sure what it was because they couldn't get too close to them. On their approach, the mother would flap her wings and turn around, full of a resolve and aggression they had not seen in her before. Zooey's body seemed full of ticks or lice or some bugs like that. Within a day, the infection spread to Franny.

The maggots arrived soon after. They were followed by crows, crowds of them. They kept their distance but cawed and flapped around, sometimes alighting on the ledge to see what was happening behind the tall plant. Zooey had learnt to fly by now, but seemed too enfeebled to try. Franny could muster merely an unsteady shuffle. Other pigeons came in to roost around the plant, as though on a vigil. The mother rarely left her chicks. The bird that Arnab thought of as the father – although he could no longer be sure given that there were so many of them, so many that the ledge seemed to be not big enough – came to visit more often. And all the time, there was the cacophony of the crows, lunging and leaving, taunting and daring the pigeons with their harsh cries.

Arnab no longer ate standing up in the kitchen. He did his homework in his own room, but in the afternoons, the rustling and flapping, the overturning of the odd utensil and the cawing, upset him. When he peeped at the little birds of whom he had grown so fond, he felt frightened: the ferocity of the crows scared him; the pigeons, so many in number, panicked yet determined, were no longer a source of curiosity or cause for delight; and Franny and Zooey, smothered and ugly, their bodies diseased, seemed nothing like the birds he had christened so recently.

'Those chicks. We can't go on like this. The kitchen is a mess. And I am worried that Arnab might catch something from all that filth,' Malini said one evening later that week. 'The filth is all over the utensils.'

'But how can we get rid of them?' Samrat asked, his voice low, something in it between timidity and apprehension.

'I know what to do.' Malini usually did.

On the way to school the next morning, she told Arnab that they could no longer have the pigeons on the ledge. She explained what they would do with the chicks. She said it in her kind but firm voice, a voice that suggested she knew it would be hard for Arnab, hard for all of them, but there was no choice but to do the hard thing. Arnab knew the tone well. He knew that when his mother used it, it meant that she would brook no discussion about the matter at hand.

'But if we leave Franny and Zooey downstairs, will the cats get them?'

'Let's hope not, Arnab.'

'Zooey can at least fly. Franny can't. What about Franny?'

'They each will have to make their own luck, just as all of us do.'

As Rakesh slid the car into its parking slot after they returned home, Malini asked him to come upstairs. She told him what needed to be done.

Rakesh was good at these things. He was fearless and dexterous. He had once killed a rat that was wreaking havoc in the Chaudhuris' apartment. The rat had eluded the watchman for three days.

Malini could not bear to watch. She went to the bedroom and put on Kishori Amonkar as Rakesh entered the kitchen. Amid the flapping and shrieking, Rakesh grasped one chick, took it downstairs, left it concealed behind the rainwater pipe. He came back upstairs, picked up the other one and left it next to its sibling. The mother had left soon as Rakesh had picked up the first chick. He did not see her when he was done with leaving Franny and Zooey downstairs.

When Arnab came home that afternoon, the ledge had been scrubbed clean. The plant and its pot had been thrown away. Silent, the boy stood for a long time and stared at the empty space. The sun glared through the window.

It seemed to him like the end of something. He did not yet know what it was the beginning of.

CHELSEA FOOTBALL SCHOOL

The lift wasn't working. This was the second time this week that it had broken down. Priyanka Dandekar had returned home to check on her son's homework, but there was no way in which, laden with three heavy bags full of groceries and other provisions, she was going to be able to climb seven flights of stairs. A repairman, lugubrious and faintly irritated, was crushing a large black ant under the heel of his sandal as he spoke to the security guard.

He said the lift would be fixed in an hour. Priyanka called Sachin on her mobile, told him to first finish his maths. She told him that she was going out again, would be back in an hour or so and then they would go through the exercise on active and passive voice together. And, oh, he shouldn't forget to heat his snack up in the microwave.

'Mum, if I am done and you are still not back, can I go downstairs and ride my cycle or play football?' Sachin asked.

'You won't have the time to do that. But, yes, if you do…'

Priyanka decided to go to the bakery for baguettes and to the ATM to pick up money. She hadn't had the time for those two errands, but now she could use this hour for them. It would save precious time tomorrow morning.

When she thought about it (and she didn't have much time to think these days; in a way, she was done with thinking), Priyanka was relieved that each of her days was filled with more things to do than she had time for. Being a working single parent required, most of all, time. And time was what Bombay – with its interminable commutes on continually traffic-choked streets – withheld from her. There was simply too much to do. And there was never enough time to do it in.

During the stupefying days after her husband's death, amid the disbelief at the suddenness of it, she had felt a kind of irrational anger towards Ajit. Why did he have to go and desert them? It had, in that initial deranging period, seemed like a betrayal. That anger was never unmixed with a sense of guilt. Why did I let him throw away that landline? Why did I not make a fuss as I had every time the matter came up till that Sunday morning? Although, who could have said that the landline would have been working that evening? It hadn't been the morning Ajit went downstairs and chucked it into the bin. And who could have said, considering the massive nature of the heart attack Ajit had suffered, that he would have been able to get up, walk towards it and dial her number? And even had he been able to, would there have been time?

Who could have said, who would have known, how would one have been able to tell ... She had to keep thinking about all this at bay if she were to not lose her mind.

Friends and family always said that she had 'picked herself up' very quickly. That she had been brave and strong and not 'gone to pieces' as some people they knew had done. The innumerable retellings of the sequence of events that led to Ajit's death begged questions – 'He had become so fit, hadn't he? He had quit smoking, hadn't he? Could it then have been the drink? He was drinking, wasn't he, that evening? Really, with these things, you never know where you are, do you?' – and the questions were always followed by lengthy anecdotes of women who knew other women who had been unable to cope with the deaths of their young husbands.

You are doing very well. You will be all right.

The way Priyanka saw it was that she had had no choice. How could she betray their son? Sachin had been closer to his father than most seven-year-old boys. She knew she could not be – as everyone started saying she was – both mother and father to him. She could only ever be his mother. And she wanted to be as good a one as she could possibly be.

The office was calling. Or someone from the office, now in a different time zone, was. This matter – of being always on call – was the one thing in her life that had not changed after Ajit's death. She had at first thought of scaling down or scaling back or whatever the term was for offering to do less work for less money. But then, she had wondered, could she bear to handle being less busy? These phone calls at all odd hours were her only link to her old life and she clung to them, even grew fond of them.

Despite her parents' entreaties, she had decided not to give up her job ('Priyanka, you need to find more time for Sachin. He will need you much more than he did before. You are mother and father' – that phrase again – 'to him now'). She had not moved back in with her parents who lived further north in Versova. She did not want Sachin's life to be disrupted and altered in other ways. She would continue to live where she had with her husband, her son would continue to go to the same school and have the same friends. Ajit wasn't there any longer, but she owed it to herself and the life that Ajit and she had built together and were so happy in, to carry on as before. It wasn't easy. But it felt like a tribute. It felt like the right – no, the *only* – thing to do.

Well, not exactly like before. The wall that Ajit had got knocked down between the two flats he had bought to create the spectacularly large and much admired living room went back up again. Two discrete flats were again created. They moved into 9B (the address they had had when Ajit was alive), and sold 9A. Sometimes, even the halved apartment they now lived in seemed too large to Priyanka. What did they do with so much space in that other life? What filled it?

Ajit's Audi went too, sold by putting up a notice on the members' board of the Willingdon Sports Club where Sachin still went swimming and for his tennis lessons. This dwindling seemed to Priyanka to be an appropriate mirror of their diminished lives. But she wasn't about to say as much to anyone. There was one item that she added to the household: she bought a new telephone set and had the landline connection restored.

She worried about Sachin all the time. The boy had been seven when his father died. He was intelligent and kind and was doing well in school. But he was prone, now that he was growing up, to bouts of moodiness and periods of sharp withdrawal into himself. He had become fanatic about sport, just as Ajit had been – Ajit had instilled in their son this love of sport – and she could see he acutely missed his father's companionship, knowledge and enthusiasm when it came to playing or watching a game on TV.

Priyanka did not care at all for sport. But she tried, for her son's sake, to get interested. She read the papers keenly, tried to keep up with the scores, made an effort to remember the names and achievements of players. She even searched online and found out what keepy uppy or a deep-lying playmaker was. But there was too much ground to cover and however hard she tried, her interest didn't appear authentic to her son.

Sachin was a true devotee. He scoffed at her shallowness. 'You are not a *real* fan, Mum. Why do you bother?' He never wanted to watch sport with her as he did with his father, treating her like the pretender she was in a part of his life that was closed off from her for ever.

And then there was the reading. Neither Ajit nor she were readers in any sense. Their apartment had some old paperbacks – thrillers Ajit had bought when he was young – and the several coffee-table books they had received as presents at their wedding, but that was that. Sachin had begun to read voraciously. He was bringing back armloads of books from the school library. The e-reader of Priyanka's iPad was in use for the first time. He wanted a Kindle of his own for his next birthday.

Often, he would buy books online and the wrapped packages would turn up at Priyanka's office, the delivery man to be always paid in cash. She realized that this new passion of Sachin's was welcome, that he was creating for himself a life of the mind that his parents never had, and would, because of it, never feel lonely without companions. But this area of his life, too, was one from which she was excluded.

Everyone said she had picked herself up quickly, but only Priyanka knew how she had not been able to put herself back together. Only she knew of her fractured mind, of her sense of dislocation. Ajit and she had loved the Darren Aronofsky film *The Wrestler*; in her anguished moments, she thought she was like the protagonist in Bruce Springsteen's title track for the film: '*a one-armed man punching at nothing but the breeze*'.

Sachin's well-being had become a sort of obsession with her. She felt vulnerable all the time, defenceless even, terrified of being destroyed all over again. She called her son every so often, just to make sure that he was okay. Sachin sometimes felt put off by that. More than once, he had let his annoyance show.

But she couldn't help herself. She kept fighting, and losing, against a rising tide of panic. What if something happened? Something irrevocable and utterly unexpected had bent their lives out of shape once. Who could tell from what angle disaster would overwhelm them again? Was there a way to avert it? What was *it*? The anxiety was a corrosive thing. With Ajit's death, the solidity that she had once felt about her place in the world had dissolved; gradually, it had vanished altogether.

The cash dispenser wasn't working at one of the ATMs, so Priyanka had to go further than she had initially intended to withdraw money. A car had double-parked in a ten-foot-wide lane off Pali Hill, causing the traffic to back up all the way to the main road in a shuddering cacophony of horns and hurled insults.

Glancing at her watch, she realized that she would reach home later than she had meant to. And after the English exercise, she needed to get dinner going. She thought of calling Sachin. No, let him be. With luck, at least the lift would be working by the time she returned.

As the car pulled in to the compound of Imperial Heights, Priyanka saw Sachin in the play area a few feet away. He had his back to her. Facing her and kicking a football around with him was a man she did not recognize. Sachin and the man were both wearing Chelsea football shirts.

Who was this man? What was Sachin doing with a stranger? How many times had she told him not to … Why was this man here? She would have recognized him had he lived in this complex. How could he have simply walked in from outside? Why was he playing with her son? What was the idiotic security guard doing? Each question a jab of panic as Priyanka, asking the driver to stop, stop *now*, tumbled out of the rear passenger door of the car.

The security guard arrived to help her with her bags and hold the door open. He seemed not in the least worried about either an imposter being on the premises or his being charged with dereliction of duty.

'Who is that man?' Priyanka almost spat out as she whipped her head towards the stranger. 'What is he doing here?'

'Madam, he lives in 3A. He moved in a few days ago.'

'Oh,' said Priyanka, the relief making her feel weak. 'Oh, I see. How long has he been living here, you said?'

'Two-three days, Madam. He came at the beginning of the week, I think. Sir is not from Bombay. But he had nearly no luggage with him when he came. But he had boxes and boxes of books.'

'Oh,' Priyanka said again. 'Oh, I see.'

Sachin had spotted her. He came towards her at a trot, his face sweat-streaked and glowing, and skipped out of her way as she bent to kiss him. He felt self-conscious these days about such public shows of affection, especially in front of people he did not know too well.

Priyanka caught him by his hand as he was about to dart away. She managed to smell his hair. Looking up, she saw that the man had not moved from where he was. He was now facing her, almost appraising her, thumbs hooked into the pocket of his jeans. He was wearing a Lampard shirt. Ajit always used to say, she suddenly remembered, that you could tell something about a person from the players they admired.

Because of his height and skinniness, his shirt seemed at once too short and too capacious for him. His hair, straight and long, fell over his forehead. He wore fashionable glasses and a faintly wry expression. It seemed as though there was some joke to which only he was wise.

He came forward and said to Priyanka: 'Very bright boy you've got there.'

He did not offer his name.

Rude, Priyanka thought, and, in turn, decided not to offer hers.

'It must appear so to a fellow Chelsea fan,' she said.

'He is very knowledgeable.'

'He watches too much football. During his holidays, he stays up for a quarter past midnight kick-off. And the Internet ... there is so much of sport out there.'

'I meant he is very knowledgeable about books.'

Priyanka felt that she had been wrong-footed, that the stranger had played this conversational gambit on purpose to discomfit her. (Later, when she would come to recall this first meeting, Priyanka would wonder whether he had been trying to wrong-foot her or whether they had simply been two strangers conversing at cross purposes or whether indeed she had been wrong-footed that evening. But that was for later.)

'Oh, he reads a lot. Even while having his meals.'

'He is on to a good thing,' he said. 'He is on to two good things, actually. Sport and books. What more could the adult that this child will grow into want?' Again, that faintly ironic expression, not quite condescending, but somehow unnerving for Priyanka. As though he had worked out that she was neither a reader nor a follower of sport.

'Mum, he is a writer,' Sachin said, prodding a finger in the direction of the man who clearly was no longer a stranger to him.

A writer? Priyanka looked at the man with renewed interest. She had never met a writer before.

The stranger gave a half smile and flapped his right hand. The gesture was less dismissive than deliberately camp. (Again, when she would later come to wonder about every detail of this encounter, she would puzzle over whether the writer had thought this was some joke she was supposed to have understood or whether he had made the gesture knowing it was a joke but one that she would not be able to get.)

Turning to Sachin, the man said: 'Do you know what the famous Liverpool manager Bill Shankley had once said?'

He paused a beat.

When Sachin didn't answer, he went on: 'Shankley said, "Some people believe football is a matter of life and death. I can assure you it is much, much more important than that."'

Sachin shrieked with laughter.

'And the great writer George Orwell' – he was now addressing both of them – 'once wrote about how serious sport has nothing to do with a sense of fair play. He called it "war minus the shooting".'

'War minus the shooting.' Sachin repeated the words aloud, after the man. 'That's really cool.'

'You are too young for Orwell just yet, Sachin, but I'll see if I can get you a book about Shankley. I might have something at home.'

'That will be awesome.' Oss-sum. These days, Sachin often dealt in the superlative which children and young adults had squeezed dry of all superlativeness by overuse.

'There is a Chelsea School of Football in Bombay,' the man said, again appearing to be addressing both Priyanka and Sachin. 'It's really very good. One or the other of the top players sometimes comes out for a week or so.'

'Yes, I know,' Sachin said. Priyanka did not know. She wondered when Sachin had found out and why he had chosen to keep this bit of information from her.

'Tell you what, Sachin, you should try and see if you can get into it.'

'It's frightfully hard to get into.'

'Well, I know someone there. I'll ask. He might be able to help.'

'Please don't go to all that trouble,' Priyanka quickly cut in before Sachin could make evident his delight at this development. 'Please.'

She didn't want to look at Sachin's face now.

'No, it will be a pleasure,' the man said. 'Really. Sachin reminds me of someone. I'd love to help. In any case, I am at home all day.'

Sachin's friends had been talking about the Chelsea School. He had read up on the Internet. He hadn't thought he would be able to get in. And now, now this writer was offering to help. He looked up at his mother.

Priyanka caught her son looking at her and touched his arm. 'That really is extremely kind of you. If you really don't mind going to so much trouble for us...'

'No, I'd like to. Let me talk to my friend.'

'All right, then. Thank you.'

'And once I have had a word with him,' he continued as though Priyanka had not spoken, 'the three of us could go there together and have a look at the set-up.'

'Yes,' Priyanka said. 'Yes, we could go there together.'

'I'll let you know what my friend says. You can then tell me when we could go.'

'Yes, I will,' Priyanka said.

The sun was low. The evening breeze was picking up. Bed sheets hung out to dry on the balconies were rippling like flags. Toeing a fallen debdaru leaf aside, Priyanka said: 'We'd better be going home. We've got English homework to do.'

'Yes, me, too. I've got some English homework as well,' the writer said. Then he grinned. Holding out his hand to shake hers for the first time, he said: 'I am Shankar.'

Priyanka introduced herself as she shook his hand.

The lift had been fixed. Shankar held the door open for them. Sachin was bouncing the football with his left hand as he went in. Inside the lift, he high-fived Shankar.

The lift sucked them homewards.

BROKEN RIBS, BROKEN HEART

It was only when he woke up the day after the day after the incident that Samrat Chaudhuri realized that he had broken a rib. He still didn't know he had actually broken two.

In Delhi on work, he had slipped while taking a shower in his hotel bathroom.

The plane had landed in Delhi on time. That, for Samrat, whose luck was such that nearly every flight he took got delayed for some reason or the other, was in itself a triumph of sorts. His room was comfortable. And because he had stayed in the hotel before, it was familiar – or at least familiar in the way hotel rooms can be. He had the whole evening to himself: in his leather grip was a new book; new music was on his tablet. Soon room service would bring up his favourite pork chops. Samrat was feeling more all right than he had felt in a while.

He had been singing aloud a song from the new Kaiser Chiefs album. He wanted to give Arnab the music when they met on Sunday. (He was still old-fashioned enough – in the days of live streaming and download, Apple radio and the cloud – to want to give his son CDs. Something to remember me by.) He was showering in the huge, gleaming, white tub, holding the telephone shower like a microphone.

When Arnab was little more than a toddler, Samrat would bend towards his son, raise his little arms, entwine his own fingers with Arnab's and do a jig on the floor of the living room to the sound of rock music playing loudly on the many speakers. Malini always smiled when Samrat did this. He hardly ever went on to the dance floor in public, in a bar or disco or even at an office party. (Actually, he hardly ever went to discos and avoided office parties if he could.) Dancing in public made him feel stupid, especially because he knew he neither had nor would he ever acquire the instinctive, natural, loose-limbed fluidity that marked out an impressive dancer on any floor. And on the odd occasion on which he had been coerced into dancing, he had looked as though he was being tormented.

Samrat couldn't recall the instant of slipping. He remembered the instant of falling, the lack of balance, his feet giving way, of his being out of control and the sense of impending catastrophe. All of this must have happened in a couple of seconds. When asked about it later, Samrat said he remembered it frame by frame, in exaggerated slow motion.

Keeling over, he hit the edge of the tub with his right side. He then lay in the bath, unable to move, unable to reach the telephone to call for help, his body motionless but convulsed with electric jolts of pain that seemed to go on and on. After what seemed to him like a long time, he got up. The pain did not relent, but the nature of pain was such that it went unremittingly on, and one began to behave as though it had always been there. Samrat raided the mini bar and waited for room service. Finding a position that did not hurt as much as other positions did was hard, but he lay gingerly on the bed, book open, the bedside lamp adjusted so that the pool of illumination was just right. When room service rang, it took him a long time to get to the door. After dinner, he doped himself up with ibuprofen and a sleeping pill. He finished all the whiskies there were in the mini bar. He did not remember falling asleep. He must have fallen unconscious.

The meeting the following day was like most meetings, and Samrat endured it as he did most meetings. The ibuprofen helped in no small measure and although he sat in the ergonomically engineered chair at an odd angle, no one noticed.

Later that day, Samrat hoisted his suitcase into the hired car, hoisted it out and then took it off the conveyor belt after he had arrived in Bombay. Every little movement hurt, but the fact that he was mobile – that he could *do* these things – told Samrat (a veteran of broken bones in the slushy football fields of Calcutta) that nothing had been broken.

When he woke up in his bed the next morning, he found that he simply couldn't move. He could turn neither left nor right. As he tried to pull himself upright, trying to make his hand, palm flat on the bed, absorb most of his weight, waves of pain broke inside his body. He felt nauseous. He could barely breathe.

Later he would say that he didn't really know how he had managed to reach the bathroom. He knew he needed to go; he knew he didn't want the maid – who had a key of her own, now that he lived alone – to come in and find him supine and in agony. And he knew that he would in any case need to get up and about even to see a doctor or get an X-ray done.

He also knew that he wouldn't call Malini. It would have been the easiest solution. These days they had arrived at a place they had imagined they would be in the weeks during which they had decided but not yet announced to Arnab their decision to separate: a courteous, mature, friendly relationship; affable, accustomed to each other, their son still at the centre of their now separate lives.

It would have been the easiest to ring Malini and ask if she would take him to the doctor, but something stood in the way. Was it pride? Was it stubbornness? Was it a refusal to let her see him this vulnerable? The pain, as he raised his arm to shave, was an animate thing. It was like a live animal inside him, twisting through him, spreading, usurping his body, wanting to emerge from where it had been trapped inside his ribs. He closed his eyes every few minutes. When he coughed his smoker's cough, it was as though his body was being wrenched inside out. Flecks of orange and red popped and swum on the inner part of his eyelids.

He walked to the intercom, fixed to the wall beside the main door where Malini had got it fixed many years ago and called Shailesh Patil. On his retirement following his widowhood, Shailesh had become a sort of solicitous senior citizen of Imperial Heights. He had more time than most and he was helpful but non-interfering. Samrat had always got along well with him. And now, with Malini and Arnab gone, and Shailesh's wife, Nandini dead, their aloneness had become a kind of bond. It had brought them together, without making them any more intimate than they had been.

Samrat did not yet think of himself as divorced. A divorce was not irrevocable, but when said aloud, it just seemed like that to him. He said he was separated from his wife. Which, given that they had not had any of the legal stuff done, was strictly accurate. Samrat had wanted to move out of this flat when they had decided to live apart. But Malini said she wanted a fresh start.

(How do you have that when what came before it hadn't quite ended?) But she wanted, she said, a fresh start and found a small flat for herself and Arnab in Juhu. It was only a twenty-minute drive from Imperial Heights; the beach was close; and when Samrat visited on Sunday or when Arnab came over early in the day on a Saturday, there wasn't much traffic. It was all right.

Once Malini and Arnab had moved out, Samrat himself had not been quite sure about how his life would turn out in Imperial Heights. Whether being where he had been for so many years – the same photographs and prints on the walls, the same sofa, the light coming in through the lattice of leaves in the same way each morning – would prolong an illusion (an illusion of what exactly?) or serve to heighten how different his life was these days.

Malini had the car and she had Rakesh to drive it. Samrat had insisted, although not for Malini's sake. Arnab needed it more than anyone else and Samrat felt reassured when Rakesh was driving the boy around. He didn't get around much in any case and the company had only recently given him a new car. Samrat had retained their old maid. Again, it was because he felt comfortable with her, comfortable with her having the keys to the flat. Savita knew his ways and could be trusted. Sometimes on the phone, Malini asked about Savita's work as though she was only out for the day and would be back in the evening to check on what the maid had been up to in the flat.

The morning after his wife had left him, Samrat had found on Malini's bedside table a book with its face down: the last thing she had read while she was here. Why had she not taken it with her? Why had he not given it back to her in all these months? He had picked up the book, snapped it shut and put it, at an angle, behind the lamp on what he still thought of as her side of the bed.

The apartment, to the casual glance, was pretty much as Malini had left it. Only, when he looked carefully, did he see the thin webs of dust at the corners of the blades of the ceiling fan in the bedroom or an obdurate circular stain on the dining table left behind by a mug of coffee. Savita wasn't as conscientious as she once used to be, but that was inevitable. He expected no better.

When he was at home, Samrat did what he could. He was fastidious by nature. He hated slovenliness. But on weekends, he hardly had the patience or the will to supervise Savita's work. It wasn't bad on the whole, he thought. He rarely had anyone round. On the odd occasion that someone stopped by, they never noticed anything wrong. Or at least they never said so or stared as if they had noticed.

Shailesh asked his driver to go slowly and carefully. Propped up by a cushion, Samrat cowered in a corner of the rear seat, his hands clasped over his ribs as though to prevent them from disengaging from his body. Shailesh had bought a Volkswagen Passat on retirement; it was a step down from the company ones he had used in the distinguished years of his career. The car was a purring, powerful beast, but the roads they were on as they threaded their way through the morning traffic into Bandra East – its tower blocks at odds with the old housing colonies on which were imprinted the stories of a previous Bombay – those roads were not ideal for the vehicle.

Each tremor, each negotiation of a pothole, each slamming of the brake, made Samrat lurch forward in pain, the lurching forward exacerbating the pain. By the time they reached the hospital, the handkerchief he had been dabbing his forehead with was soaked through.

The orthopaedic surgeon nodded at the X-ray as if satisfied with what he saw. 'Two fractures, Mr Chaudhuri,' he said in the manner of one imparting good news that he had known was coming. 'The bones have moved away from each other. What did you do after the accident?' He smirked.

'All that suitcase hoisting aggravated it. Tch,' he said, after Samrat had recounted his journey back to Bombay from Delhi. 'You had merely a crack to start with. And now this.' He gave Samrat a rib belt (a broad, tight thing with Velcro at either end, bulky and immensely itchy when worn) to wear at all times, prescribed rest – as much as possible – and more painkillers.

'A month, say, or six weeks and you can go back to exercising.' He looked Samrat up and down. 'You do exercise, don't you? You must. A brisk twenty-minute walk every day cuts the risk of cholesterol by thirty per cent.'

The doctor stroked his protuberant belly and wrote out a receipt for his fees. Samrat said nothing. He wanted to ask the doctor what he did for exercise. The Woody Allen line came to him: 'I don't pump iron, I pump irony.'

When Savita came into the flat at noon, she was startled to see Samrat wearing shorts, the rib belt over his T-shirt, sitting at the dining table, smearing mayonnaise on a piece of bread. He smiled at her.

Eating and drinking were the two things he could do without being acutely aware of his broken ribs. Otherwise, even sighing was agony. He had thought he wouldn't tell Malini and Arnab. But he saw there was no way in which he would be able to meet Arnab on Sunday. He would have to tell them that he would not be at Juhu to pick him up. He imagined his son's face, his brows knitted in baffled disappointment. If he didn't tell them the truth, how long would it be before he saw Arnab again? Would Malini visit on an impulse? Would she bring Arnab with her?

Samrat slipped the new Kaiser Chiefs album into the CD player. He unscrewed the top of a bottle of Blaxman Estate Chardonnay (for reasons unknown – and unknowable – to him, his bootlegger had been dealing only in south Australian wines for the past two months), arranged the olives and goat cheese on a plate, laid the toothpick beside them and lowered himself into his favourite armchair.

The days were long now. Twilight descended grudgingly and through the windows of the living room the western sky remained charcoal grey with smears of washed orange.

Samrat punched Malini's number into his mobile.

He shifted around. He was getting skilful in working his way around the pain, skilful in not minding its gnaw, but still yelping with each movement that sent the live animal corkscrewing through his body.

He hated being fussed over. When Malini would ask him more than once if he had had lunch in the office, when she would bring his medicine to him on the occasions he had been ill and insist that he have it right away, he would be brusque. He didn't know even now how genuine that brusqueness had been. Had she known at the time? Now that there was no one to fuss over him, now that he did not want to let on about his accident to his son and his ex-wife (no, the wife he was only separated from), he felt he might have been grateful if someone was around to ask him how brutal the pain was.

Malini picked up on the third ring. 'How are you?'

'I'm okay. How are things over there?' Over there. Twenty minutes away, but it was over there, and not here.

'Things are fine. Arnab has qualified for the state-level final of the spelling bee. I got the email this afternoon. How was your Delhi trip?'

This afternoon? It must have been at least four hours ago. Couldn't she have texted to tell him? Why did he have to find out *so late*? Imagining Arnab's face creased with delight at the news and knowing that he had not been there, imagining that he had not asked to immediately speak to his father and tell him, knowing that *he* had not called him, or made Malini do so, imagining and knowing all this made Samrat pulse with something that was in equal parts bitterness, anger and remorse – and yet none of them, really.

'Oh, Delhi was the usual crap,' Samrat said. 'Look, there's a problem with Sunday. I can't make it.' He wanted the conversation to end swiftly.

'Oh, dear. Arnab will be gutted.'

'Let me speak to him. I'll explain to him.' Let me speak to my son. My *son*.

'Baba, I am in the spelling bee final. I made it.' Arnab was speaking in the tone that was usually accompanied by a no-big-deal shrug, as though this outcome had been an inevitable one, but Samrat could sense his son quivering with pride and excitement.

Why had he not asked Malini to call him?

'Well done. I am very proud of you. You are the best boy in the world.' Samrat scratched at his rib belt. It did not ease the itching beneath it; he could feel the dampness of sweat accumulating.

'Are you bringing the new Chiefs album on Sunday? Navjyot downloaded two of the songs, but I said you'd got the album for me.'

'I've got the album for you. But I won't be able to go see you on Sunday.'

'What do you mean, Baba?'

'I've got to go in to work. There is an important meeting. I have to, Arnab. Sorry.'

A sound of something, not quite snivelling. Something like deep disappointment made audible, made its way to Samrat's ears down the mobile phone network. The boy cried too easily these days. When they had been together, he had hardly ever done that – even when he had once, while slicing a banana, cut his thumb open with the kitchen knife after being told to never touch that damn thing.

'Arnab?'

It wasn't his fault, he thought, that he had broken two ribs, but Samrat felt guilty. Guilty for what his life had become, for disappointing his son, for how his son's life had changed, for what he had made his wife go through, for not turning things around when there still was time, for letting it all come to this.

'Arnab?'

'Oh, Baba ...'

'If you get Ma to send Rakesh around, I could send the CD over. Or I could send it by courier to you.'

'It's not that, Baba.'

Arnab hung up.

Samrat finished the wine before the dinner he had ordered from the Lebanese takeaway had arrived.

He remembered his rages. All those monomaniacal rages when he had been married. All the things he had said that he had not quite meant, but meant them enough to have said them. All the things he had not stopped himself from saying when there was time. The rages exacerbated by drink. That had happened with Harold Pinter too, he had read. And Mailer and Vidal and Styron … So this was what he had in common with great writers.

The great writers were his heroes, not the rich advertising professionals who were on the creative side and deluded themselves by thinking that they actually *did* create things other than misconceptions. Not to speak of the richer philistines on the business side of the company who thought that the creative guys were cogs in the wheel and that they constituted the wheel.

Malini had cried, in the aftermath of his rages, so many times. He had pretended that he was drunk, that he was asleep, had kept still, had pretended – even the morning after – that he had not heard her at all.

The rows. His parents, hers, them. Was it worth it? And now this.

He had told her, when they had decided to get married, that he was hard to live with. He had told her that he was impossible to live with. She had managed. But she couldn't after a point, not any more.

Why had he done it? And now, with the pain lancing through him like a plane through clouds as he reached for a glass that no longer had any wine in it, this was what he was left with.

Why did he feel like crying?

Samrat held his chest, his heaving chest that hurt so much to heave and wondered if his broken heart would ever mend.

THE SHITPOT SALESMAN

We haven't met before, have we? Not that it matters. I won't, like the Rolling Stones, be so bold as to say, 'Please allow me to introduce myself, I am a man of wealth and taste.' I'll keep it simple and direct. Hi, I am Manish Chandiramani.

Had you known me (I don't know, perhaps you *do*), you might have thought of me as a bourgeoisie moneybag. That's what my wife, Sunita, had called me. Or that's what she had thought of me when we first met. She told me this later – after we had fallen in love. Hah.

On the other hand, you might have envied me. I know a lot of people who do. Look what I have to show for myself. I have this huge, lovely flat in Imperial Heights, one of the poshest apartment blocks in Bandra, one of the poshest parts of town. The current market value would be six crore at the very least. I drive a BMW 5. (I have read in the papers that of all his cars, Sachin

Tendulkar loves his BMW 5 the most.) At Imperial Heights, where your worth is index-linked to which car you own, this earns me serious respect. I live in 14A and I have often thought of what it might have been like to break down the wall between 14A and 14B to merge them into a single apartment of double the current size of one. Ajit Dandekar on the ninth floor had done just that. But we were here too late. 14B had been sold by then and however easy it might be to afford the merger of two apartments, that course of action is now blocked.

I have a beautiful wife. I have a daughter who is turning out to be a prodigy on the piano. You would have had every reason to envy me, to want to be like me, to desire to get where I have got from where I had started. Self-made man, many people call me. With grudging respect, I think. Well, I know a great deal about the self as well as about making it.

I am a salesman. Well, I have a fancy title and all that. I am called an executive director. Some of them call me 'Eee Dee' in the office. They are the ones who want to be extra respectful by not addressing me by my name. The office happens to be a very large German corporation with tentacles across the world. I am the ED of its South Asia operations.

But in effect I am a salesman. I know that. Why, I am proud of it. Why shouldn't I be? I see no reason why everyone has to be an intellectual. Sunita is one. She teaches English literature at the university. Most of her friends are intellectuals too – academics, journalists, writers. There is a writer who has moved into Imperial Heights. Although, from what I hear, Priyanka Dandekar sees rather more of him than Sunita does.

I like describing myself in an uncomplicated way. I have no pretensions. You know what I sell? Shower heads. Commodes. Sinks. Taps. Bathroom fittings. I am the one who makes the big deals. Get them to sign on the line, raise a toast and that's another hefty annual performance bonus. I love that. I am good at pushing stuff, at being persuasive, at telling clients why what we have is precisely what they need. And I know my wares and my company as well as they can be known. That's how I rose to be 'Eee Dee', you see. And by devoting my life – yes, my life, that is not an exaggeration – to my company, my job, my work. Is there any other way that you know of by which this sort of thing can be accomplished?

My job requires me to travel a lot. Nearly every other week I am off to some part of the world or the other. Everyone needs high-end commodes and shower heads these days. It's exhausting, all that travel. I complain about having to travel so much, about the logistics of travel, all those long waits at airports, the many-hour-long flights.

But I'll let you in on a secret. I don't mind travelling at all. I like it, even.

No wait at an airport is unbearable as long as the lounge has a decent bar. And I enjoy being served with fancy crockery and cutlery, drinking champagne from a proper flute, reclining in my reclining seat, sleeping as though I am in an advertisement for an airline (as though I *am* an advertisement for the airline) while the hordes in cattle class sit cramped and uncomfortable, eating off their trays placed on those precarious, tiny fold-out tables. Being in an aeroplane shows me what I have left behind. It reminds me again of how far I have come.

What's not to like?

I have colleagues who say that the loneliness of travel gets to them. It doesn't to me. I am driven by my work. Even in Bombay, I spend most of my waking hours at work. Or around work. I love the adrenaline rush of making the big deal (travelling somewhere *to make* the big deal), the king-sized beds in five-star hotels, shopping, expensive restaurants and bars in Europe and America. With my iPhone and my iPad, I am never lonely.

Well, there is another reason why I like travelling, but more of that in a minute.

The thing is, I have got used to being on my own, got used to not being lonely when I am on my own. It wasn't always like this. When Tanvi was little, I would be home by seven in the evening. I didn't need to travel much on work. On particularly hot and still evenings, no breeze to stir the curtains, Sunita would make iced tea with mint leaves, the reddish-brown colour of the tea bleeding into the cubes of ice.

Even weekday evenings allowed us time to watch films. Or some shit show on TV. Or listen to music. We always had dinner together. We didn't live in Imperial

Heights in those days. We had a modest but airy apartment in a building with an unprepossessing exterior in Andheri East.

Things were very different. But of course you can sense that.

My spectacular skill in selling commodes changed all that. It put me, as an email from the HR head at the time said, '... on the fast track to growth'. My ascent in the company wasn't so much a climb as a zoom up the ranks. GM; AVP; VP; ED (I vaulted over the Senior VP rung altogether). Having conquered the acronyms of the middle and higher reaches, I now stand near the very peak. In my sight is the very summit: the CEO's job.

When I was spotted as someone on the make, enhanced responsibilities entailed enhanced travel. My job was to persuade clients in Delhi or Bangalore that our shit pots were the best and that our taps were what they had wanted all along. I would make them believe that they came to such knowledge only after they had listened to my presentation.

There was novelty for me in all this. But I really did mind the travel because it took me away from home. I missed Tanvi. I didn't want to be away from Sunita so much.

As my reputation within the company grew and my remit increased, the boundaries of travel expanded. One year I was feeling thrilled that I was being put up at the Taj Palace in Delhi; not too many years later, I was simply taking for granted the Calvisius Caviar Lounge at the Four Seasons in New York.

The world started shrinking. I was accumulating so many air miles that we did not need to buy tickets when we travelled abroad on family holidays.

Somewhere between what I call my national and international phases of travel, I began to enjoy the whole thing. Or was it not between but into the first year of travelling overseas? Or was it during the second? In hindsight, it is hard to tell. Who knows? I really don't know whether there is one particular moment in which such transitions take place.

I do know, however, that the more frequently and the further I travelled, the less I saw of my family. The iced-tea-and-movie-and-music-and-TV evenings were long gone. I wasn't much at home. And even when I was in Bombay, I began to see Sunita and Tanvi only on weekends.

Tanvi's school started at seven o'clock in the morning. Sunita would leave with Tanvi at a quarter to seven. They would be out of the house well before I had woken up. Having dropped Tanvi to school, she would carry on to the university. She picked Tanvi up from school, brought her home and went back to the university. She returned – as she always used to and still does – in the early evening. The earliest I would be able to come back from the office would be ten in the night. Often, it would be later. Work spilled over. The journey back took long. Frequently, there were clients visiting from abroad who needed to be entertained. By the time I got home, Sunita and Tanvi would be asleep. I ate on my own, the TV on, and collapsed into sleep.

The weekends on which I was in Bombay, I slept a lot during the day, recovering from the week or preparing for the next overseas trip. Often, I would be working from home. Tanvi became busier: she had piano lessons, she had piano practice at home, she had maths tuition, she played basketball. Sunita would ferry her to and from all these things, watchfully overseeing Tanvi's evolution into the well-rounded, well-spoken, well-read, admirable person she wanted our daughter to become.

On Saturday and Sunday evenings, we either went to a party at someone's place or invited people over. These parties always ended very late, especially on Saturdays, filled, towards the time of departure, with either fake backslapping, hugging bonhomie or loud, rancorous arguments among the guests – the friendliness and the bickering were both brought on by staggering quantities of duty-free alcohol.

I can't remember exactly when we fell into this routine. But we did and that is how it went on. I wasn't, as I said, home many of the weekends of the year in any case. We became three people who inhabited the same flat.

No, that's not quite right.

On hindsight, I think that it was I who turned into the odd man out. I missed watching Tanvi grow up. Did I miss not seeing Sunita as much as I used to? I am sure I did. I remember that during certain long plane journeys – looking forward to the big deal, adrenaline and champagne coursing through my bloodstream – I often thought about how distant we had become from each other, how different a family we were at that time, compared to the one we had once been.

But I had a job to do. A job at which I was evidently excelling. A job that got the BMW 5, the flat in Imperial Heights etcetera, etcetera. You know all that by now. I had a job to do and I did it. It was – as people in the world of sales and marketing love to say – a zero-sum game. And I was playing by its rules. No, no, don't judge me. I simply can't stand that.

So. The time has now come to tell you about the other thing that makes travel worthwhile. The women. Do I see your lip curl in disgust? Your brow furrow in disapproval? Please, please, we are all adults here. I can't bear your moral righteousness.

As I said, just because I am telling you all this doesn't give you the right to judge me. Keep your censure to yourself.

Yes, the women. When was the first time that I was unfaithful while I was travelling? It was in Berlin. That I remember very well. Oh, and that it was winter. Not a great deal of the encounter itself has stayed with me. It should have, I suppose, given that it was the first time. But it hasn't and that's all that there is to that. Besides, in this bit, I intend to merely state the facts – or the facts of what I remember.

Berlin with the trail of the Wall running through its heart. The grandeur of the Brandenburg Gate. The edginess of Potsdamer Platz. The stately lime trees on Unter den Linden. The wind whipping the river Spree. The spectral feel of winter. All this I remember.

I won't tell you her name. Protection of privacy, I hear you snigger. Call it what you will. I won't tell you what she looked like either. You can make up an appearance if you like. No person looks the same to two people. Yes, yes, objectively, we can talk about height and body shape and features and colour of eye or hair. But what a person really looks like is how she appears to the other. It is all a question of perception. Of feeling, too. And impulse and circumstance and motive and many other things. I won't go into any of that.

The deal had been sealed. The toasts had been raised. I was feeling – as I do on these occasions – triumphant. Everyone – as they do on these occasions – had had way too much to drink. At some point during the party, it had become clear to both of us that we would depart together.

I assume that you know how these things go. I do now; at that time, though, all this was new to me. So if I want to be really precise, I shouldn't say that it became clear to *both* of us. Perhaps it was clear to her. To me, it seemed like a madly exciting possibility, a possibility made all the more thrilling because it was both forbidden (till then, that is; I suppose I had been my biggest discourager) and unprecedented for me.

Leaving the party together, we went to Café Einstein on Unter den Linden. The soft globes of light on tall, slim cylindrical stands. The rich, red depth of the upholstery. The lime trees through the slatted blinds of the large windows. I enjoy being at the Café Einstein although it is a touristy place with grumpy waiters. I'd been there before. I've been there since. That time, we had a coffee each. She had hers with a shot of grappa. The coffee must have been good. It usually is. But I don't remember. I recall that it did not make me any less drunk. The grappa might have made her drunker.

With a sense of inevitability, we went to my hotel room. Now, now, don't be prurient. Don't ask for details. I am not about to divulge any. Just the facts are what you get. Or my recollection of the facts, such as they are.

There was a great deal of fumbling and groping and exhalations and exasperation at things getting in the way. For me, there was a great deal of unfamiliarity – not just with the person, but with the whole situation. That made everything more awkward. It couldn't have been enjoyable for her. I don't know how she remembers it.

We never even exchanged email addresses or phone numbers. Afterwards, we did not talk much. She did not stay over but, collecting her things, left the room, gently pulling the door behind her. Her heels did not echo. The corridor was expansively carpeted. My room faced the lifts.

I am trying to be as matter of fact as I can about this, but I must confess that I thought of nothing else all through the next day and the flight home. The fear made the inside of the plane seem colder. The panic made me feel ill.

What had I done? What would happen now?

But I'll tell you something here. There is nothing like a long flight to calm you down. After a few hours (no, it was more than a few), the panic began to abate. My mind made swift adjustments to new situations, sizing up the possibilities and the strategy. My job had taught me to do that.

Shortly before landing in Bombay, I had arrived at the following conclusion: We didn't even have each other's phone numbers or email addresses. There was no way in which we could or would be in touch. Life wasn't an Erich Segal novel. Okay, what I had done was wrong, very wrong, but then it was an impulse. No emotion had been involved and I remained dedicated to my daughter and wife (with whom I hadn't had much of a conjugal relationship lately) and it might be best for everyone to simply accept all this and move on.

Which brought me to the other key question. Whether to tell or not tell Sunita. Coming clean, I knew, was the *right* thing to do but convenience often has more on its side than rectitude. What was there to be gained from confessing? It was, after all, just the one lapse. Things would go on as they were. Things must go on like that. And she'd never find out. She couldn't, could she? How would she?

I know how I sound but don't make me tell you again to keep your outrage to yourself. I am at least being honest here. I wasn't to know at the time that this would not be *just the one lapse*. And, given that you may well ask later, the other lapses changed nothing in my way of thinking.

I didn't tell her.

But you know what, the movies have it wrong. My misdemeanour did not send me back into the arms of my wife with new-found love. It did not make me pay Sunita any extra attention. I did not bring her flowers or lavish presents; only the customary bottles of duty-free and a Chanel No 5 because she had run out and had specifically asked for it.

We simply carried on as before. Travelling, working, going to or hosting parties on the weekends on which I happened to be in Bombay, not seeing one another during the week and Tanvi growing up, to most intents and purposes, almost in a single-parent household.

After that first occasion, something changed inside me. I became alert to the possibility of infidelity every time I travelled abroad. And I was taken aback by how easy opportunities were to come by.

These were encounters where neither party expected anything other than the physical intimacy of a single occasion. Nothing other than mutual attraction and expediency was involved. No strings were attached. Sometimes, it was quite fun.

On a couple of occasions, once on the Reeperbahn in Hamburg and once in the red-light district of Amsterdam, I purchased sex. You saw what was on offer, you knew exactly what you were buying for those brief minutes. The nearly naked woman behind the glass. Bored, reproachful, seductive, trying hard, indifferent, doing her job. The crush of tourists. A swift transaction, the red curtains drawn, in the small downstairs room.

There was guilt, yes, as there was self-loathing, but the combination of the two was not strong enough to prevent me from yielding again when temptation presented itself.

It's the nature of addiction. Who am I to assume that you know nothing about that?

In the past few weeks (or has it been longer? I search in vain again for the particular moment), things have been a little different at home. When I say home, I mean between Sunita and myself.

Tanvi has been just as preoccupied and self-absorbed as ever; we greet each other and converse like people who used to be best friends once and still have something left over to be able to pick up and carry on a conversation even though they don't see much of each other. I love my girl just as unconditionally as I ever did. And she seems to still be fond of me, seems to love me even, need me, after a fashion. I feel grateful for that.

No, that's not it. Something is now different between Sunita and me. From whenever it is that it has been different, I am now certain that things are coming to a head. You can always tell – if you have lived with someone for so many years, even if you haven't been living with her as much as you once used to – that something is wrong.

It's not just the testiness that manifests itself on the phone. It's not what preceded the testiness: the extra effort I noticed that she put in finding time for us as a couple (and being unsuccessful at it). It is not the point-blank refusal to go to a Saturday night party that had been planned weeks ago. It is not the hostility she exhibits as I prepare for another trip. Or perhaps it is all of this and something else.

I can't put my finger on it.

All I know is that something is lurking somewhere and that a flashpoint is imminent. I don't know what it is or the direction from which to expect an attack. That makes me feel vulnerable. It makes me tense and very worried. I know that I am not in control of this situation.

What is it? She couldn't have found out, could she? How the fuck would she have done that? It's impossible. Can you guess? Do you know? Has she told *you*?

THE PROFESSOR OF ENGLISH

We weren't, unlike some of our neighbours, one of the first people to buy an apartment in Imperial Heights. Rather, we moved here when the building was a few years old. We bought our flat from a family that was migrating to Canada. It took me a while to accustom myself to the idea that this luxury was now my natural element.

It took me more than a while to realize that moving to Imperial Heights was at the same time a beginning and an end.

Oh, look, I'm so sorry. Here I am, prattling on, having dived right into the middle of the story I want to tell you and I haven't even introduced myself. I am Sunita Chandiramani. I live in 14A with my husband, Manish, and our daughter, Tanvi. I teach English at the university.

And, at the moment, I think that my life is falling apart. (Perhaps that has been the case for a long time. You could well accuse me of wilfully ignoring that fact. These days, I accuse myself of having done precisely that.)

I don't know if you have ever met Manish. If you have, he must have given you the guff about his being merely a salesman, how he loves being uncomplicated, anti-intellectual etcetera, etcetera.

Don't be fooled by any of that. It's an affectation of his, a sort of inverse intellectual snobbery. Manish is the executive director in a reputable German company. He is accomplished, intelligent and quite a gourmand. If he wants to be, he can be charming and quick-witted, he can make you laugh. It was all that – and the fact that he was handsome ... well, he still is – that made me fall in love with him all those years ago.

In many ways, he is the opposite of the brash braggart that he would like you to believe he is. 'Who would have thought,' I had said in our early days, 'that someone who ought to be an aspiring bourgeois moneybag would have such a genuine passion for Schubert?'

We were able to buy an apartment in this building because of the spectacular success that Manish was at his job. And the more successful he became, the more he was driven towards even greater success. The success consumed him. It also thrilled him no end.

And me, too, in the initial phase of the success at any rate. I must try to be truthful here.

Why would anyone complain about the lifestyle that it afforded us? Having said that, all this opulence mattered less to me than it did to Manish; I was content with how we had lived in Andheri. But, if I am to be truthful, I loved everything once we moved here.

The trouble was, Manish and I were rarely able to enjoy this plenitude together. I remember one day shortly after we arrived here. It was early on a Monday evening and I was reclining on the curved raised platform that goes up to the foot of the tall windows. I had chosen the cushions and their covers myself, burgundy with blue silk trimmings, matching the curtains and the eiderdown. Tanvi was away at her piano class. Our maid Savita had made dinner and left early. The quietness in the apartment was a presence.

The windows, running along the breadth of the wall, were open. Through them, I could see clouds edged with purple, with mauve, with gold. The sun, huge and mellow, was on its way down. The sea breeze had set up. The green outside was luminously quivering.

Suddenly, there was the doorbell, insistent, sounding louder than usual. I was startled. The security guys downstairs allowed no one up without checking. It would be a while before the driver returned to pick up the car keys so that we could go to collect Tanvi from her lessons.

It was Manish.

'How did you manage to get home so early?' I asked. Something like this hadn't happened in months.

'Would you like some green tea? I was just about to put the kettle on. We can go together to collect Tanvi. She will be thrilled.'

Manish held my eyes for a few moments. Again I felt the deep quietness within the flat; I heard the curtains in the living room swish in the breeze. In those instants, I think I saw in Manish's eyes a wistfulness that vanished almost as soon as it appeared.

'A sudden client meeting has come up in the evening. We have to entertain them. So I'll have to go all the way to the Oberoi. I just came back to shower and change into a suit.'

Within a quarter of an hour, he was gone. He returned – as he usually did – after Tanvi and I were asleep. When I left to drop Tanvi to school and go on to the university, Manish was asleep. I saw him next on the weekend. And that's because he wasn't travelling that week.

I know of couples for whom the relationship works because it is conducted over a distance. Absence, if not making the heart grow fonder, papers over cracks that might have appeared between them. For us, it was just the other way around. Absence was just that: the lack of presence, emptiness, making us remote from each other, excluding the one from the other's life.

As Manish continued his pole vault into the highest echelons of his company, the strain began to grow. I don't recall that many arguments or fights. (What, really, was there to say? It was the job, it was the job, we both knew and, as he never stopped reminding me, without the job, where would we be? Back in Andheri East in the other flat and that, simply put, was no longer an option. It wasn't, not to him.) I just remember the growing silence; first, the silence of absence; and then the increasing silence in each other's presence.

We began to socialize more than we had done before. Being in the presence of others mitigated – or at least concealed – the tension between us. Besides, we were both good at appearing to be a happy couple in company.

I am not sure exactly when that ploy collapsed. I do know that it went completely out of hand.

We started by going to parties once a fortnight, perhaps once every three weeks. Before long, I found that we were either visiting someone or other or hosting every weekend that Manish was in Bombay. I said that we should stop going on Sundays at least; that there was school the following day and starting the week in a state of sleep deprivation was not what I wanted.

This occasioned a huge shouting match, with Manish saying that while he slaved for us and endured the tedium and exhaustion and loneliness of such frequent long-haul travel, his wife couldn't even bear to give him company on the weekends on which he managed to be at home. It wasn't that, of course. I said so. I said all I was suggesting was that we keep each other company at home on Sunday evenings. But no, he wouldn't have any of it. Manish became furious, saying he enjoyed parties and if he did, given that he wasn't around all that much, why could I not stop being prissy for fuck's sake and come along to them?

It went on for a very long time. I held out. In the end, I gave in.

It was a mistake.

Those were train wrecks of weekends. After a while, he moved the parties to our house on Sundays. Tanvi could at least go to bed on time. We accepted every invitation that came our way: from friends, colleagues, neighbours in the building, acquaintances, colleagues of acquaintances, acquaintances of colleagues.

Oh, those weekends … Manish would work from home most of the day, the bedroom door shut, emerge to have lunch and then sleep off the tiredness of the week in the afternoon. At first Tanvi complained about not being able to show her father this; about not being able to talk to him about that; about looking forward to doing the other with him and not being able to.

Then she stopped complaining. 'Dad's always very busy' became the reality she accepted and yet when they found brief spells between the busyness, they got along with the sort of cheer and intimacy that Manish and I had begun to relinquish.

He would get wasted at those parties. On more than one occasion, he had embarrassingly loud altercations and stormed out and I followed, making apologies, my smile a little lopsided but still there. No, no, please don't take offence, he didn't mean what he said, you know how it is, the pressure of work, and then – my hand miming a bottle being raised to my lips – oh, just too much of it, sorry, sorry.

Often at these parties there wouldn't be anyone of Tanvi's age. On such occasions, she would refuse to accompany us. (I fear that seeing her father so spectacularly drunk had gone some distance in putting her off although I have to admit that, in spite of being forthright and opinionated, I never heard her blame her father for this.) She would have her own friends over and, failing that, she would spend the evening by herself.

Somehow, I found the vision of our daughter eating a TV dinner on her own on a Saturday night upsetting. But by then, we were caught in the whirl of parties, trapped and being spun around like clothes being tumble dried.

I should have said no. I couldn't bring myself to. I was weak, I feared an outburst, I deluded myself into thinking that, yes, if Manish wanted me to go with him to these parties, I should, especially because he wasn't around for such long periods.

We all make mistakes, don't we?

Manish, I am certain, knew what was going on in terms of our relationship. He couldn't have *not known*. I think he was intelligent enough to know that the job was corroding our marriage, but he didn't really believe in or want something else so strongly as to be able to break free from the job.

If you talk to him, he will, of course, say that he was incapable of doing anything about it. He had a job to do. Yes, he did and the being away had to do with the job, but not everything did. I brought up the weekends because the weekends – the ones that we could have spent as a family – need not have been like this; notwithstanding the job, we could have held on to them.

They might have saved us. Or, as you will learn in a moment, not.

In those months – it could have been longer; it's hard to be certain without pinning down when exactly things started to go awry, precisely when the strain appeared, how much the gap was between the tension arising and my taking note of it – in those months, I had often thought of quitting my job. I had wondered if that would help.

I would be able to spend much more time with Manish, see him every morning. Perhaps even, if I napped in the afternoon, be there when he returned from work and stay up and have dinner together.

I considered it and then rejected the choice because I could not be sure if merely being around would offer a solution. Or perhaps I say this now because that is how I have worked it out for myself with hindsight, with the aid of the knowledge that I am now in possession of. At the time, perhaps it was nothing quite like that; perhaps it was just that I didn't want to give up my job badly enough, feared interrupting (worse, terminating) my career.

The further Manish and I began to drift away from each other, the more I began to cling to Tanvi.

I became obsessed with her studies and her piano lessons. I wanted her to excel in her studies, get away from this apartment and this city, go to university abroad and make her life over there.

I became fixated with the idea of her safety, telling her to be careful at all times, to immediately report any gesture or advance she found unsettling. The gang rape of a twenty-three-year-old student in a bus in Delhi had unleashed waves of shock, fear and outrage across the country and the newspapers and television were reporting every day instances of assault on and violation of women and young girls.

Whether it was school or piano lessons or basketball or a birthday party, I made sure that I accompanied Tanvi everywhere. I scheduled my lectures and day around hers. I ferried her to and fro, never allowing her to travel only with the driver. My friends and colleagues laughed at me, calling me a control freak. It wasn't as though the driver was untrustworthy. It was just that I kept thinking, who knows, one moment, a single moment of madness or provocation and we'd be left with a lifetime of anguish on our hands.

I couldn't imagine what it might be like to live with that sort of culpability.

One Wednesday morning in late March, the weather having already turned warm, the humidity making you want to wring your clothes while they were on your body, Shireen Chavan suggested that we go out for coffee. Shireen, who specializes in Jacobean drama, is a colleague at the English department.

No, she is more than that; she is a close friend and the only one in whom I had confided about the downward spiral in my marriage. I was happy for the invitation. For the past week or so, Shireen had been distant; she had stopped phoning to chat, quickly gathering her things and leaving if the opportunity for a private moment arose in the staff room. One morning between lectures, I had caught sight of her looking at me intently, a puzzled, odd look and she had turned away towards the person next to her when she saw that I had seen her watching me.

I had been intrigued, but I didn't know if I wanted to ask her. Was something wrong? Was it my imagination? I'd decided to wait for a few more days. And then here she was, suggesting that we have a coffee, so things must be as they ought to be.

As it turned out, they weren't – not at all.

The conversation in the car was desultory, and I could sense that there was something – something to do with me – that was bothering Shireen. Even after we arrived at the café, she appeared to be restive and nervous, fanning herself with her hand in the air-conditioned air while ordering, dabbing at her lip with a napkin, drumming the tabletop with her fingers.

'What is it, Shireen?' I asked. 'Why can't you sit still? What's going on?'

'Oh god, what can I say? I have been thinking about it for days now, wondering how to tell you and now, well that's why I suggested we come out.'

She told me.

She tried neither to soften the blow nor heighten the drama. She told me the story straight.

Shireen had been to a conference in Barcelona the week before last. On her third evening, returning very late from dinner with fellow attendees, she was picking up her room card from the front desk when she had seen Manish get into the lift with a young, white woman. She was certain that it was him. He had steered the woman into the lift. The doors had closed. And then, as another guest intending to go upstairs had pressed the button before the lift could start, the doors had opened again. He was at this moment facing Shireen. The woman and Manish had their arms around each other's backs. She got a good look, three or four seconds at least, as the occupants of the lift rearranged themselves inside it. There could be no mistake. It was him all right. It was one in the morning.

Shireen began to cry, loud sobs that drenched the small paper napkins the café had provided.

'I didn't know how to tell you,' she kept saying.

'I am glad you told me. Thank you.' I patted her hand, as though she was the one for whom calamity had struck.

That was how the crazy period began. Could it really have been Manish? One couldn't be absolutely certain, could one? Yes, one could. Shireen would not have spoken about it had there been even an iota of doubt. One look, a second one, three or four seconds. Perhaps it was a colleague. But one doesn't enter the hotel lift in a foreign city with one's arms around one's colleague at one in the morning. Or one doesn't if one entertains merely colleague-like feelings towards her.

I knew that Manish was in Barcelona when Shireen had gone for the conference.

So was it what it seemed it was? Well, how could it be otherwise? Accepting that image – and, therefore, the truth behind that occurrence – happened to be only the first step of the agony.

The next step was the nearly continual, maddening question to which only one person could give me the answer: If it had happened once, had it happened again – or before? If this was what had taken place in Barcelona, how about New York, Munich, Amsterdam, Berlin, Paris ... the world seemed like a spinning plastic globe on which was mapped the terrain of Manish's infidelities.

And then there was the third stage. (I say first and second and third phases as though they were all discrete, set apart from one another. But I suppose that is not how it was. It is how I have constructed my experience to have been. In reality, they must have all been one roiling, churning mess of fear, panic, anger, betrayal, shame, inadequacy.) The third phase then, just to break things down, was this: Could he not have told me? When it happened for the first time, shouldn't he have confessed? Didn't he owe me that? And, did he not say anything because he thought he would get away with it? That I would never find out?

Was that what he had thought?

I screamed at Savita in those days for not enough reason. I was absent-minded. I forgot my phone in a taxi one afternoon when going to pick Tanvi up from school. I still remembered to schedule my lectures in such a way that I could accompany Tanvi at all times.

One week, when Manish was not travelling, I took leave from the university so that I could spend more time with him. (Was this merely spending time with him? Merely being around more?) He didn't talk much. Certainly he mentioned nothing of other women or guilt. I tried to see if there was something I could do to unlock him.

No, it didn't work.

Nothing worked. Nothing works. I need to have it out now. He is the only person who knows. But will he tell me the truth? The truth and the truth about why he hadn't told me the truth.

I have to confront him. It is the only thing for me to do. I have to know now. I have to know. I have to sort out my life. And ours.

EXCHANGES

From: Shankar_Shivaraman@gmail.com
To: dpriyanka@yahoo.com
Date: Saturday, June 30 at 1.46 AM

Dear Priyanka,

The day we first met, I had told you that Sachin reminds me of someone. Maybe you don't remember. Well, he reminds me of myself when I was a boy.

Let me try and explain. I went to see my first test match at the Chepauk in Madras when I was his age. (The city was called Madras then. The stadium was called Chepauk. Neither name remains.) I had gone with an uncle of mine. At the stadium, I made friends very quickly with the other adults around me. They were very impressed by how knowledgeable I was, how I knew statistics stretching back to before I was born, how well I read the game, how mature the pleasure I derived from it was. They said so and I had felt very proud of myself. My uncle told my mother about what the other spectators had said and she was just as proud of me. Sachin has that effect on sport-loving adults. He really is very impressive.

When I was his age, there was no TV and no Internet. You could play cricket or football or tennis as much as you liked, of course. But otherwise, as a fan, there were so few ways in which you could cultivate your passion for sport. There was the radio, yes, and black and white sport magazines. But if you were so inclined, a child in those days could be just as passionately keen about sport as a child is now. I was as devoted then as he is now.

I wonder how that could be. Does that say something about children? Or about passion? Or about the imagination? I am in the habit of asking questions which I don't know the answers to.

Sachin's appetite for reading mirrors mine. Mine as it is even now but, more importantly, mine as it was when I was first discovering, as a child, the world that words reveal. He reads closely, and well. It is such a thrill to see that quality in a boy. Few of us know that reading is an acquired skill. One needs to be taught – or one teaches oneself to – read well, and closely. Only then do books speak to us as they are meant to. Books speak eloquently to Sachin. Has he finished *Haroun and the Sea of Stories* yet? There is no hurry; it's not that I want it back right away.

You are very lucky to have him. He is a wonderful boy. I mourn his loss – and yours – and I believe he will turn out very well.

It was a pleasure to visit the Chelsea School with you the other day. I hope Sachin will thrive there. I have been housebound the past week. When work isn't going well, I can barely leave my desk. For some writers, the problem is solved by taking one's mind off it. But I sit and not work and try, keep gnawing away at the stuff till things get a little better. It's a torment, this business of writing, full of self-doubt, but being a writer is to be reconciled to a life of not being satisfied. It is a perk of the job.

I shall be down soon enough to play some keepy uppy with Sachin. And should he need help, I'd be happy to help him with his English. Although having said that, I must confess that a writer can be a dangerous teacher of English. What he imparts may not be what the school curriculum and exams demand. So, on second thoughts, perhaps that isn't such a good idea.

Take care.

With all good wishes,

Shankar

PS: I am very glad that Sachin and I are both Chelsea fans and that we both worship the cricketer after whom he was named. Otherwise, we would have had violent disagreements. And that would have been no good thing.

PPS: If you go to guardian.co.uk – the website of London's *Guardian* newspaper – you will find the link for an e-book titled *Chelsea's 20 Defining Games of All Time*. Sachin will love reading the book, I think. Perhaps you would want to buy that for him? I would love to, but he needs to download it on his device.

From: dpriyanka@yahoo.com
To: Shankar_Shivaraman@gmail.com
Date: Wednesday, July 3 at 7.56 PM

Dear Shankar,

Thank you for your help. Sachin and I are both grateful for it. He is enjoying himself at the Chelsea School. He has become a huge fan of yours.

I know nothing about writing or writers. I am not even much of a reader, but I suppose you must have guessed that. So I can't imagine how hard your work is. I am sorry to hear of what you call your torment. I hope things will get better soon.

I do know that you are well known as a writer. Sunita Chandiramani from 14A told me that. She said that you have won a big book prize. She was on the interview panel of society members when you wished to rent your flat. She said Samrat Chaudhuri from 12A supported your bid because he has read your work and admires it. Samrat is a big reader. He always has his nose in a book. Even when he is in the car! You should meet him. See, you have two fans already in Imperial Heights. Sunita also said that several people on the panel were against letting you live here because you are a single man with what they call 'no fixed source of income'. They meant a proper job in an office. Although there is someone here I know – I won't tell you who it is, you will have to find out for yourself – who doesn't have a proper job. He lives off the rent from the flats his father bought. But that is a 'fixed source of income'. Plus, he owns the flats and is not a tenant.

Tenants, especially if they are single or have odd working hours or are Muslim, have it hard in Bombay. Have you noticed that there isn't a single Muslim family in Imperial Heights? And did you know that there are certain apartment blocks in Malabar Hill in which you will not be able to rent an apartment if you eat meat? Those building societies are controlled by Jains and they will not allow in anyone but vegetarians. We are better off in that respect here, I think.

Sunita also said that two of the three bedrooms in your apartment are kept locked and so your landlords treat it like a 1-BHK apartment. Does it feel strange to live in an apartment like that?

Sachin is doing well in school. He topped his class in both English and maths. And he could barely sleep from excitement after the Wimbledon final. He woke up all groggy on the Monday morning after. Even in the morning, he could not stop smiling from the memory of the final. He has grown obsessive about sport and I sometimes worry if this will affect his studies.

Like Samrat, he reads in the car. He reads with a torch when he is travelling in the evenings. I have bought him the e-book about Chelsea games. He loves it. Thank you for the suggestion.

Hope you are enjoying Bombay.

With best regards,

Priyanka

From: Shankar_Shivaraman@gmail.com

To: dpriyanka@yahoo.com

Date: Saturday, July 7 at 9.12 PM

Dear Priyanka,

Don't knock living off rent. I do that myself.

Many years ago, I used to work for a newspaper. I like to think that I was good at my job. At least my bosses used to say so. But I wanted – from as far back as I can recall – to be a writer. I didn't want to be the sort of writer who wrote only in newspapers. While at the paper, I did write an unpublishable book.

The pressure in the job was relentless and I realized that, for me to give this writing business a real go, I needed to devote much, much more time than I was able to. While journalism taught me discipline and the skill of writing to frenetic deadlines, I knew that I needed to develop the stamina and endurance it takes to produce a book. Journalism does not teach you to be patient.

Around that time, my father, who had worked very hard all his life in the civil services, bought me a large flat in an expensive area in Chennai. Armed with that asset, and determined to live off its rent, I packed in the day job.

Over the years, it hasn't always been easy. It isn't easy, especially after a certain age, to count money all the time, to not be able to be self-indulgent on a whim. But I am not complaining. I am always aware of how lucky I am because I know other writers who don't have the luxury of giving up the day job, who suffer the agony of having the material and the talent and yet not the time to write the books they want to write. I am my own patron and that is good enough for me.

I live in what my landlords call a 1-BHK because that is the only thing I can afford in Imperial Heights. They have kept their own stuff in those two rooms and gone abroad and so they charge me for the use of a single bedroom. I rather like the arrangement. I often spin fanciful stories in my head about what there might be beyond that door. I am in Bombay to research a new book and it is convenient for me to live in this neighbourhood. I live on my own. I need little space. I am happy in this flat.

I do make some money from my writing, but that isn't really enough to live lavishly. I write the sort of books that are never in any danger of making my publishers and me rich. Failure, damage, heartbreak and loneliness interest me as subjects. And books born of those particular fascinations are not likely to be terribly happy ones, are they?

Which is why I am so glad to hear that not only has Mr Chaudhuri read my work, but also admires it. I am not exactly Chetan Bhagat. Had I been, you would have known of me. And the interviewers on the panel over here wouldn't have worried about my not having a 'fixed source of income'.

You told me that you had never met a writer before. Well, I wouldn't recommend meeting writers. I must warn you that they tend to be competitive, egotistical, solipsistic, ruthless, manipulative and predatory. I meant predatory in terms of what they think can be turned into books. (Some are predatory in the other sense too, but that is not a universal trait.) They think of everything as material, everyone as fair game for the purposes of their work. The English writer Graham Greene once said that all writers have a splinter of ice in their hearts, which is to say that they have a streak of ruthlessness that they put to the service of their art. One must be – as another English writer I admire once said in an interview – one must be abnormal to want to be an artist, to want to create something.

The other day, I saw a man sitting on a bench on the pavement that runs alongside Bandra talao. I don't know if you have noticed those benches. Each of them has a metal plaque that says Ravindra Giriraj Trust. Perhaps the trust gets people to maintain them because the benches are oddly clean amid the surrounding squalor.

I saw this man sitting on one of them, facing the road with his back to the lake. He appeared to be very old although it was hard to guess his exact age. His left leg was amputated from the knee. His crutch lay beside him on the bench. He was wearing shorts, the colour of which was impossible to tell. The scrap of cloth that covered part of his upper body had once been a shirt. He had scabs all over his body. Some of them were covered with crusty, dried blood. The bus I was on was stuck in a snarl, so I watched him out of the window. He sat still, mute, almost immutable. Even his eyes didn't move.

I don't know why I wanted to tell you about this.

Write soon.

All the best,

Shankar

From: dpriyanka@yahoo.com
To: Shankar_Shivaraman@gmail.com
Date: Sunday, July 8 at 4.32 PM

Shankar,

What do you mean when you say that writers 'think of everything as material, everyone as fair game for the purposes of their work'? I don't want to be in any book of yours. I am not material, okay? The man you described seemed to be in a terribly sad situation. When we see such things, we realize that our troubles aren't as huge as we think they are. Thank you for telling me about him. It made me feel lighter. But does that mean I am deriving pleasure from his misery?

How would a writer answer that?

I won't ask Chetan Bhagat.

Cheers,

Priyanka

Aug 14, 11:21:36 AM
From Shankar
To Priyanka
Would you like to meet for coffee at the Barista near Shoppers' Stop at 6.30 p.m. today?

Aug 14, 11:28:12 AM
From Priyanka
To Shankar
Cnt do dat. Sachn nd I r gng swimming. Come 2 d club @ 6.30? Coffee nd swm?

Aug 14, 11:58:29 AM
From Shankar
To Priyanka
Ah, that will be lovely. Thank you. I shall be under the foyer of Willingdon Club at 6.30 p.m. I haven't gone swimming since I moved to Bombay. See you.

Aug 14, 12:13:41 PM
From Priyanka
To Shankar
K. C u.

Sep 09, 2:34:19 PM
From Shankar
To Priyanka
Thank you for sending over the bowl of lasagne. It was delicious. I feel so stuffed that I can barely work. Hope Sachin enjoyed it. I intend to make beef pickle over the weekend. Shall send some over to yours. Why the weekend? My week is no different from my weekend. I don't know. There is something expansive about a Saturday morning.

Sep 09, 2:42:07 PM
From Priyanka
To Shankar
Lasagne wsnt dat gr8. Dnt lie.

Oct 30, 8:13:27 PM
From Shankar
To Priyanka
Have you told Sachin? He is a perceptive boy and is at an impressionable age.

Oct 30, 8:16:53 PM
From Priyanka
To Shankar
No. Wats thr 2 tell? U dnt undrstnd.

Oct 30, 8:21:48 PM
From Shankar
To Priyanka
Sorry, it's all up to you, of course. I didn't mean to meddle.

Nov 1, 4:46:36 PM
From Shankar
To Priyanka
Shall we meet for a coffee at the Café Coffee Day on Carter Road this evening? I can be there at whichever time suits you.

Nov 1, 5:01:22 PM
From Priyanka
To Shankar
I tld u we cnt go on meetng like dis so near 2 home. I tld u why. Cnt keep mssging abt dis. Wll email.

From: dpriyanka@yahoo.com
To: Shankar_Shivaraman@gmail.com
Date: Sunday, Nov 5, at 10.44 PM

Shankar,

I have been meaning to write this email for several days. I have been putting it off because I wanted to think through about what I have to say. It has been great to get to know you ever since you moved in here. I have enjoyed your company. Sachin admires you. We are both very grateful for all the ways in which you have helped us.

But we can't go on meeting each other in cafés in this neighbourhood. It's not the same as talking to each other while Sachin and you are kicking a ball around downstairs.

Shailesh Patil saw us at the Barista on Linking Road. He mentioned nothing to me. But Sunita did ask. I may have imagined it but I think I saw something in her eyes. More importantly, we can't be sending each other the dishes we cook through the maid. Savita works in five households here, including in yours. People talk. Whether we like it or not, people talk.

Sachin will get dragged into all this. I will not allow that. Nothing should disrupt his life. I am most committed to that one thing.

I hope you will understand.

Priyanka

From: Shankar_Shivaraman@gmail.com
To: dpriyanka@yahoo.com
Date: Sunday, Nov 5 at 11.16 PM

I am confounded by your obdurateness. How can you let a child rule your life?! How can you let what other people say influence what you do?

S

From: dpriyanka@yahoo.com
To: Shankar_Shivaraman@gmail.com
Date: Sunday, Nov 5 at 11.22 PM

Shankar,

I am not letting what other people say influence my actions. I am doing what I think is right. Sachin is my first priority. I had no idea that you were so self-centred and obstinate. Do you ever think of anyone but yourself?

Priyanka

Nov 6, 7:02:23 AM
From Shankar
To Priyanka
I am sorry. I am so sorry. I switched my phone on this morning and read again what I had emailed you last night. I am ashamed of myself. Please forgive me.

Nov 6, 8:42:07 PM
From Shankar
To Priyanka
I have been thinking about this business all day. You are right, of course. I have to find a way. I shall write to you in a few days. Take care. Apologies again.

Nov 7, 6:37:42 PM
From Shankar
To Priyanka
Do you want me to find a way, Priyanka? Please reply.

Nov 7, 9:46:39 PM
From Priyanka
To Shankar
Up 2 u. Find a way if u wnt 2.

From: Shankar_Shivaraman@gmail.com
To: dpriyanka@yahoo.com
Date: Tuesday, Nov 20 at 12.41 PM

Dear Priyanka,

I miss autumn. Or, as my friends in America call it, fall. The flaming leaves; the trees being stripped; the whisper of goodbye to summer getting louder and louder till it is a cry and winter, with all its sombreness, wraps its arms around us. Bombay has only two seasons, doesn't it? Hot and wet. You can feel the seasons change, the year grow older, in Delhi and Calcutta. Only Chennai is worse.

I have decided what I must do now. I have made up my mind to move out of Imperial Heights.

Ever since I decided the days have been a bit of a blur. Finding a suitable apartment in Bombay is manic enough; finding another one within months of arriving at the first is worse. My landlord isn't too pleased because he will have to go through the exercise of getting hold of another tenant. Not many families fancy the idea of living in a flat with two of its bedrooms locked up. And not many single people fancy spending as much on rent as he charges. The broker is delighted. When I saw him smile at the prospect of his commission, I smiled as well.

But everything is sorted now. I am moving to Borivali. It's a much larger flat (three bedrooms, all of them accessible) and I have not yet thought about what I shall do with all that space. But it is a nice flat, and it is in a well-appointed building complex (swimming pool, gym, mini supermarket). I suppose I will be able to make my existence as hermetic as I like – or, as need be, depending on the circumstances.

I realized also that it isn't strictly more convenient for me to research my book if I were to live in Bandra. Borivali will do, as will just about any other place in Bombay. I find all kinds of excuses to not get my work done, or take longer than I ought to – and I am, at least for the moment, determined not to allow living in Borivali to be one of them.

The place has one undisputed advantage. It puts a huge distance (and not just in terms of miles) between Imperial Heights and me. No one from Imperial Heights is likely to go for coffee at one of Borivali's cafés. As the broker said, when people from over here have to go to that part of Bombay, they say they need a visa. To me, that's the best thing about moving to Borivali.

My landlord at Imperial Heights had put in something called a lock-in clause of a year in our contract. Which means that because I am moving out after six months, I shall be obliged to pay him the rent for the remaining six months of the year. I must confess that, once made aware of this clause, I had thought a lot about whether I should last out another six months in Bandra. But I reckoned that it would be silly to let Imperial Heights get in the way of things. Silly to bicker and feel wounded and cause pain when it can be so easily avoided.

I want to give my best shot to what I'd like to believe is a new start. I want us to have a fresh start. Six months seemed too long to wait for that.

Write soon. Better still, call.

Yours,

Shankar

OH, TO BE IN ENGLAND

1. I am writing with great pleasure…

Samrat was a compulsive checker of emails. The nature of his job had at first demanded it. And then, who could tell when exactly, it had become his nature to open emails as soon as they pinged in, to respond to the ones that required a response as soon as he had read them. Often, the emails were ads for Viagra or notifications of his having won thousands of pounds in lotteries abroad.

Malini had banned the phone from the bedroom. But now that they no longer shared the bedroom, Samrat's phone had come to lie next to his pillow. He told himself (although no one had asked) that he needed it to tell the time. Malini used to wear her watch to bed. With the backlit screen of the phone, it was easier see what time it was than by taking his own watch out of the drawer and, half stupefied by sleep, squinting at it. The clock that used to sit on the bedside table had broken down months ago. Samrat had made no move to have it repaired.

11.46 p.m. The curtains leaked no light. A car horn sounded, unremitting, in the way horns often do in Bombay because drivers love keeping their palms or thumbs pressed on the horn, but its wail was muted by the twelve floors the sound needed to travel up. The air conditioner thrummed, maintaining in the room the fierce chill that Samrat preferred. He drank from his son's old school water bottle (its narrow mouth a great help; he did not spill water on himself even if he was drinking with his eyes closed), turned over on his stomach and clicked open the email.

Dear Mr Chaudhuri,

I am writing with great pleasure to inform you that, from an exceptionally strong field of applicants, you have been selected as the recipient of the David Freeman Fellowship.

May I be the first to congratulate you on your very well-deserved success. Our department of media studies will be delighted to welcome you and hope that we can make your visit a stimulating, productive and memorable one.

He speed-read the rest, skimming, wanting to get to the end of the email and wanting to go back to the beginning again, not all of it sinking in yet and the operative part of it already making him want to shout out aloud.

> I will be sending ... My understanding is that your stay will be timed for a two-month period sometime between the beginning of April and the end of June ...
>
> Thank you for your patience ... If you have any immediate queries ... Once again, may I offer you my heartfelt congratulations ...

Would he call Arnab now? 11.51 p.m. The boy had school the next day. What was he doing? Would he call Malini? No, let it wait till tomorrow. He would hug this to himself for the rest of the night. But he wanted to tell someone he had won the fellowship. Arnab and Malini were the only people who knew that he had applied.

So. Two months in a quiet university-and-cathedral town in the south of England. Two months with Arnab in the English spring. Two months to do nothing but take a few classes on creative copywriting and the Indian advertising industry; to give a few public lectures; to 'engage with life on campus' and to be left pretty much to himself.

All of a sudden, he missed the weeks of waiting for the news to come through. It ought to have come at least a fortnight ago. *We had an exceptionally high volume of applications to process ...* He missed the agony of not knowing if he would get the award because it seemed to him now, in the cold cocoon of his room in the middle of the night, that with the knowledge that he had won the fellowship, the thrill of acquiring that knowledge – the thrill that he had been so keenly anticipating and the thrill that had been kept in abeyance over those long weeks – was over once and for all.

He had applied because he wanted to get away. He had not been on a holiday ever since Malini had moved out, he had not – despite his and Malini's determined efforts – seen as much of Arnab as he would have liked to. He had asked Malini before he applied that if he won the fellowship, could Arnab come with him to England.

'Why are you asking, Samrat? It will be wonderful for him to go.' And she had touched his hand – such an occasional gesture these days, so occasional that it seemed precious – with the old familiarity, the old friendship that separation had not eroded.

He had asked if she would come. 'You could come for a week or something if you like.'

Looking out of the window of her new home as pigeons took agitated flight from the sill, Malini had said, 'No, I don't think I'd want to do that.' Then, turning back to Samrat, looking him in the eye, she had said, 'I really, really hope you win this. It will be terrific for both of you.'

To Samrat, the idea of the David Freeman Fellowship was not so much to do with how it would 'significantly contribute to his growth as a professional' or how his presence on the campus 'would open for students a window into advertising in a different culture and consumer market'.

To him, the fellowship was a phenomenal gig. Someone was paying for him to be able to spend in a beautiful place more time with his son than he had ever been able to.

He could not sleep. Samrat fired up his laptop and, using Google maps, roamed on his own the streets of the town in which he would live for eight weeks with his son.

2. What time is it in Bombay now?

Heathrow he knew well. He was familiar with its urban sprawl, its queues and announcements and directions, its nervous energy and busyness that on occasion collapsed into chaos. Don't keep luggage unattended. Way to Heathrow Express. Way to the Piccadilly Line. The tracery, like veins, of the tube lines in small folded maps in front of the ticket counters. Passengers arriving on ... The enigma of arrival, the business of onward journeying.

This is where he had landed on previous trips to England. This was from where he had sometimes taken connecting flights to Europe. London, the city that images on the Internet never prepared you for, the city in which the world had converged, not so much the capital of a former colonial power as a nation state, this London he was intimate with, the place that an English acquaintance of his called a collection of distinctive villages, Islington as unrecognizable in its mores from Clapham as Asansol was from Karjat.

But as the train skimmed through the rolling downs south of London and pushed deeper into the countryside,

Samrat found that he was a stranger to the England he was about to inhabit.

A church steeple in the middle distance, foregrounded by sheep, leisurely and portly, grazing in a meadow. Villages with names such as those in Larkin's poems. The circular top of a stone castle, grand and remote. Bridges over fast-running streams, their waters silver shards that gleamed and quivered in the sunshine. Oblongs of light and shadow on fields of ancient green. And white faces, only white faces, getting on and off at stations, politely apologetic, apologetically polite. Thank you very much. Sorry about that. Yes, please. There you go. Thanks a lot. Cheers.

His body clock disrupted but his mind trying to absorb and adjust to so many new sensations and images, Arnab sat by the window, looking out, looking back in, scrutinizing every new arrival, each carry bag bearing the name of an unfamiliar department store – Waitrose, Tesco's – looking intently, barely able to sit still and asking, asking questions of his father to which the answer often turned out to be 'I don't know'. Samrat marvelled at his son's energy and stamina, at how his good humour was intact after such a long flight, at his lively curiosity in the face of the unfamiliar.

They sat facing each other with a table, strewn with possessions, between them. Samrat kept an eye on their luggage, which stood near the door of the train. Two huge suitcases tagged HEAVY; one of the tags had torn at the top right hand corner in all the pulling and wheeling. He had wanted not to sit side by side but opposite his son so that he could gaze at him, memorize and imprint on his consciousness Arnab's each little gesture, each inflection of his voice, the way in which he gave a thumbs-up sign when pleased with something or to indicate assent and approval – all the things about his son that were now in front of him with renewed and heightened familiarity.

'Baba, how much longer to go?'

'Less than an hour, I should think.'

Samrat looked up again at the electronic board displaying the ticker tape of stations along the route. Two more stops to go. He was an inveterate worrier. He asked again the man sitting next to him with a copy of the *Daily Telegraph* if the train would go to the town they were bound for. 'Yes, yes, it will,' the man said, jerking his head up at the electronic display of stations rolling in front of them.

'What time is it in Bombay now, Baba?'

'One twenty-five in the afternoon.'

'How can you tell? You have not yet changed the time on your watch.'

'No, but I'll tell you how to work it out.' So this was the first thing that Samrat had to teach his son on arriving in England. How to add four and a half hours to the time it was in England to find out what time it was back home.

The boy widened his eyes and raised his brows. It was his gesture to convey how impressed he was with his father's knowledge of such things. 'Wonder what Ma is having for lunch,' he said.

3. The Bates Motel

It was a three-storeyed, eighteenth-century, stone house situated across the road – appropriately named College Lane – from the university's main campus. The larger of their two rooms had a bed, a sofa, an armchair, a table with a desk lamp on it, a circular dining table for four. Mismatched furniture, bought at jumble sales, but not so much worn as lived-in, comfortable. The smaller room had a bed, a chest of drawers and two built-in wardrobes. The kitchen was tiny but would do for them. The bathroom was not en suite; they had to pad along the carpeted hallway to reach it. When they looked out through the windows of the smaller room and the kitchen, they saw, across the lane used by more cyclists and joggers than motorists, the rugby and football fields of the university, like an invitation. Through the window of the other room was dense foliage, trees of varying heights receding into the middle distance, the nature of their green varying, depending on how far away they were, dancing motes imprisoned within the bars of sunlight that fell through the gaps in the branches, the brightness of the green changing as the light altered.

The walls were so thick that there was no TV signal. On discovering this, the university had taken away before their arrival the television set it had got for them. There was no wireless Internet connection. But the Internet worked with a dongle and, in certain parts of the flat, mobile phone reception was more than adequate.

Looked at from the outside, the house looked gaunt and vaguely forbidding. 'The Bates Motel,' Samrat said on their first evening as he cooked dinner.

'What's that, Baba?'

'It's the name of a hotel, sorry, motel, from one of my favourite films. I have the DVD at home. We'll watch it together when you are a bit older.'

'Have you watched it with Ma?'

'Yes, but she never quite liked it. She found it too scary.'

'Oh, I like scary,' Arnab said, reaching across to pass to his father the bowl of eggs he had whisked.

A flat for Mr Chaudhuri, Samrat thought. A new home in a new place for a few months. If only it could feel like a true new start.

4. *I can't walk like this*

Easily and swiftly they slipped into a routine. Samrat would rise, make tea, wake up his son and they would go off, half a mile either way, to the nearest corner shop to buy milk, eggs, the odd grocery item, bread (the fridge was too tiny to be stocked for even a couple of days) and – this happened every day and this was the main purpose of the morning walk – a copy either of the *Guardian*, the *Times* or the *Independent*. The *Daily Mail* and the *Daily Telegraph*, Samrat noticed, were by far the most popular papers.

All the papers were available in the university library, but Samrat, unlike many of his colleagues at the university, derived a keen sense of pleasure from reading the paper over breakfast and carrying it around with him during the day. The papers were so much thicker than the ones in Bombay and so much better produced. He kept hearing – even in a seminar he had attended recently at the media studies department – that newspaper circulation in England was plummeting, advertising was dwindling and yet, the papers went on. Were they thicker and even better previously? How did they manage to carry on? And how long would it go on? Surely, there was a lecture in it somewhere. He must look up the figures.

After breakfast, he would settle Arnab down with his schoolbooks and walk across the paved path that skirted the football field to the university. There he did his gig: the odd lecture, the tutorials, the occasional presentation of a paper. When he returned at lunchtime, Arnab would, every day, be waiting at the window of the smaller room – the room Arnab had made his own with an annoying disarray of clothes and shoes ('Why can't you put back in the wardrobe stuff you take out? Why do I have to do it for you?'), books stacked on the bedside table, pencil boxes yawning with their contents more out than in and a teddy bear in a red scarf (he really was too old for that sort of thing) that Malini had given him on his third birthday – he would be looking out of the window, waiting for Samrat to become visible as he came through the knee-high gate that stood between the fields and the road.

If Samrat was late, Arnab never remarked on it. If he was hungry because it was past his lunchtime, he never said so to his father.

In the afternoons they read, sitting beside each other on the sofa. Samrat helped his son choose books from the public library. Sometimes he read out to him – not children's books, but poetry he had borrowed from the university library. This was the bit that Arnab enjoyed the most. It took him back to when he couldn't read and his father would read children's books aloud to him. Samrat chose wisely; even if Arnab did not understand all of the poetry, there was always something – the rhythm, the setting, the subject, striking images – that would grab his attention and hold it.

There was no TV, of course, and Arnab sometimes watched the BBC's daytime programmes or some sport or the other on the iPlayer. On most days, they went to kick a ball around on the football field, Samrat teaching his son how to chip the ball, how to trap it as it came chest high to him.

Samrat ran out of breath in less than a quarter of an hour. He had put on a great deal of weight in the time since Malini's departure. He hated this fact and yet did nothing to combat his growing girth, hating even more the people who mentioned how much weight he had gained in recent months.

The only thing he did to not aggravate his sense of self-loathing was to avert his face from a full-length mirror (inside shops, shop windows, at home, in hotels or restaurants) whenever he came across one.

But if Samrat wanted to stop playing, Arnab wanted to go on; fifteen minutes was too little for him. 'I want to rest and read a book now,' he would snap at his son – and regret snapping no sooner than he had done so – and stretch out on the grass.

'Baba, are you angry?'

'No, I want to read I said.'

'Can we play for a few more minutes? Please?'

And Samrat would heave himself up and start again, scowling, but determined to let his son have his way. But something would seem to have jarred the rhythm of their play and the initial companionableness and excitement could never be restored the next time around.

If, of an afternoon, he had things to do at the university, Samrat would take Arnab along with him, leaving him in the library or allowing him to sit at the back of the room during a seminar. On occasion, he would leave Arnab at the university's music department where a charmingly eccentric head of music (in a top hat and a three-piece suit) would encourage the boy to practise on one of the department's many polished, finely tuned violins.

Thrice a week, they would walk across the common at the back of their flat, past the theatre, through an underground subway to the cobbled pedestrian precinct in the shadow of the cathedral in the centre of the town. Arnab would have an ice cream, licking off the chocolate flakes with deliberation till he grew, squealing with glee, a moustache of melted chocolate that he would not let his father wipe off. Samrat would have tea and scones. They would go to the Marks & Spencer and lose themselves, giddy with the delight of the shopper who finds himself in his element, among the refrigerated varieties of meat and fish, the chilled juices and wines, the chocolates and asparagus and prunes and peaches.

Despite having grown fat, Samrat would walk at his old pace, which was pretty brisk. Arnab was barely able to keep up. It was easier for the boy to do so on pavements, amid the crush of pedestrians swinging their shopping bags, when Samrat would be obliged to slow down and weave his way in and out of the columns of shoppers. But striking out across the common, which comprised half the journey, with such a lot of room for manoeuvre, Samrat would pick up pace and begin to really hit his stride. Arnab would keep putting his hand into the pocket of his father's jacket, tugging at him, pulling him back, slowing him down.

Without being fully conscious of it, Samrat would take his son's hand out of his pocket. He would deliberately slow down a bit. After a few moments, again perhaps without being fully aware of it, his stride would lengthen. And Arnab, to stay in step, would again, put his hand inside his father's pocket.

'I can't walk like this,' Samrat would say.

'I can't walk like this,' Arnab would reply.

This happened not more than thrice, but the fact that it did occur in the early days of their visit, gave Samrat pause for thought. He made sure that it did not happen again.

Samrat made dinner early, but they could never agree on when to eat. Arnab would begin to feel hungry around eight o'clock in the evening, but his father would be disinclined to sit down to eat before he had finished his bottle of Pinot Grigio. Unlike his English colleagues, who ate early and continued drinking till late into the night, Samrat had never been able to slough off his very Indian habit of treating the wine as an aperitif, of finishing a sizeable amount of drink before sitting down for dinner. Not that he did not enjoy drinking wine with dinner, but that had to be a sort of top-up, consumed only after he was satisfied that he had already drunk as much as he wished to before eating.

'I'll eat a little later. Why don't you sit down first and I'll sit with you at the table?'

'I want us to eat together, Baba. I don't want either of us to eat alone.'

'It's hardly alone, Arnab. You can sit with me when I eat later too.'

'No, but that is not eating together. It's not. Ma and I always have dinner together.'

On some days, Samrat would give in. Meals were a pleasure and it made the day worthwhile – the trip worthwhile – to see how eagerly Arnab devoured the honey-glazed ribs of pork, the Thai curries, beef casseroles with basmati rice, the rainbow trout in hollandaise sauce that Samrat prepared. He was pleased to find that he had rediscovered his touch. When he lived on his own, he rarely cooked.

But on occasion, his obdurateness would manifest itself and nothing that his son said would budge him from the decision he had made to eat later. On those evenings, sitting at the table, reading as Arnab ate, he found it difficult to meet his son's eyes.

They spoke with Malini on the phone every day. Rather, Arnab did. Samrat came on the line about twice a week or so. Watching the boy – animated, expectant – talk on the phone, it was brought home again to Samrat how unprecedented this occasion was, how unique. Despite that, or perhaps because of that, he could not do away with the idea that this experience was somehow incomplete, dismembered, like a photograph from which a particular element has been carefully excised. He wondered how far they had come from their family holiday on the east coast of America three years ago. He wondered if there was a way back.

5. *The chaffinch and the starling*

They were city boys, both of them, at home only with the ordinariness of the sparrow and the pigeon and the crow, the iridescence of the odd parrot arrowing through leaves, the keen-sighted wheeling of the kite or the eagle (they could not tell the difference; they did not know that the kite had a pointed wing and the eagle a broad one). So their means were always going to be inadequate in the face of what they encountered in this town.

Samrat always wanted to know the names of things and Arnab had inherited this. They kept asking people how to tell a copper beech from an ordinary one or an oak from a willow. On one occasion, Arnab shrieked with delight on seeing a weeping willow (he had never got over the name which he had come across in the Enid Blyton books he had outgrown several years ago).

But the birds were what really fascinated them. Sweeping, soaring, cheeping blurs of colour, mobile and expressive, still and deliberating, so many of them, hopping around in the trimmed lawn beside the cathedral in the centre of town or a constant presence beneath the tree (the oak tree, they learned soon enough) behind their flat, adding blobs and flashes of brightness to its dense, reassuring green.

The public library had an exhaustive collection of books on local architecture, history and the garden birds of England. And they chanced upon and bought, in the Oxfam shop on the high street, along with another soft toy that Arnab was too old for, several copies of *Bird Life*, the magazine brought out by the Royal Society for the Protection of Birds.

It wasn't long before they could tell the chaffinch from the starling and, while gasping with pleasure at their dramatic colours, deduce from their size if what they were seeing was a blue tit or a great tit. Logging on to the website of the RSPB, Arnab read about how to make bird cake.

He wanted to try.

One evening, they warmed up lard, added – just as it said in the instructions on the website – grated cheese, raisin, bird seed and peanuts and squeezed the mixture together till it attained a certain consistency. They had to then put it in the fridge for an hour to set. Arnab kept looking at his watch and opening the fridge door every so often to check on the progress.

'Be patient, be patient.'

'I am being patient, Baba, I am just checking on it.'

Samrat got up from the armchair and decided to bring the bird cake out. He was going for a refill of his wine in any case. 'All right. Let's put this out, then.'

Arnab took the used pot of yoghurt in which they had put the mixture and, carrying it with the solemnity and purpose of a priest carrying a grail, put it on the ledge outside the window of the larger room. For as long as there was light, he stood by the window, waiting for a bird to come and alight on the ledge, for it to have a nibble of the cake they had made. From time to time, Samrat looked up from his book to see his son still there, his silhouette getting smudged in the gathering dark, his shadow flickering on the floor as the day died.

Arnab refused to be distracted from the bird cake. He began to study in that room. When Samrat returned from university, his son wasn't waiting at the window, watching out for him to make an appearance through the gate that led on to the road.

Two days and not a bite.

'Why don't the birds come, Baba?'

'They will, you'll just have to be patient.' Patience. It was the thing you had to teach a child most. It was the one great thing you learned yourself from being a father.

'They are all there. I can see them on the grass. They fly past. But they don't touch our cake.'

'They probably can't tell. They are not used to bird cake being there, Arnab.'

'But why?'

'Have you heard the term "birdbrain"?'

The boy shook his head.

'It means someone who is not intelligent, someone who has no brains. Not all birds are intelligent, you see. That's why they can't spot your cake.'

'But migratory birds are intelligent. They fly those huge distances every year and don't get lost.'

'Ah, but these ones' – said Samrat, with the relief of a lawyer clinching an argument – 'these ones are not migratory birds.'

They looked at each other across the small dining table, a vividness in the quality of the light outside making the contours of the leaves sharply distinct. They both remembered the pigeons in what used to be their home in Bombay. They both thought of the life together that they no longer had.

Neither told the other about this.

6. *Extracts from a diary*

24 April, Sunday

What a day! What a day! Oh, boy! Had a pub lunch. Sunday roast beef. Yum, yum. Then went to the fun fair on the common (huge field actually but they call it a common here) behind our flat. Lots of rides. The ghost train was spooky. The huge slide was superb. Did it over and over again. Did some bird watching. I am getting to know the names of the birds. Baba has got me books with pictures and names of birds from the library. We also bought magazines. We will make bird cake for the chaffinches and starlings and blue tits soon.

11 May, Wednesday

Today was a good day. Baba did not go to the university at all. Had to study in the morning but all the sums were correct. Took a bus to a sandy beach called West Wittering. It was very windy.

The wind bent and nearly blew away Baba's umbrella. The beach huts were all shut. There were nearly no people. Sometimes it was cold. But it was sunny. I loved it. I wrote and drew on the sand with a pebble. This is what it looked like.

15 May, Sunday

Lovely game of footie today. Baba is really good. He has a strong kick and he can chip and trap and dribble. I am learning. I am also learning how to take penalty kicks and to save them. We played with mini goal posts today. The best thing was that I made two footie friends. Two cool boys. Alex and Phil. Alex is a fantastic player. I scored a goal! Whoa! Will play again with them tomorrow at half past six!

28 May, Saturday

Dear Diary, I am very sorry that I have not written much. I have been lazy. But I have also been busy. We have been travelling! We have been to lots of places! Went to Portsmouth and Arundel and Brighton. I loved Brighton the best. It was sunny and the sea was beautiful. The water was too cold for swimming. I tried. But I could only dip my toes. And Diary, the most exciting, most exciting thing was that we went on a CARAVAN HOLIDAY. Yay! We went to Wales.

It was near the Irish Sea. It was marvellous to live in a caravan. Perfect but tiny like a doll's house. I also won a prize in a drawing competition with other children. And another one for collecting the most beautiful sea shell on the beach. Quality shell, quality shell, they kept saying. I found that funny. The only thing was that the phone was not working and I could not speak to Ma for three days.

3 June, Friday

Our trip is nearly over. We will go home soon. Dear Diary, I don't know how to write this. I will miss these times so much. I will miss being with Baba. He can get angry but he can be great fun. He is more fun than angry. That's what I think. Or he is like that only with me. But I am happy that I will see Ma again. Nearly two months I have not seen her! And what a time I will have telling these stories to friends in school. They will see that I have got better at football! Oh, Diary, I would have loved to stay a bit longer here if we had all been here together. We won't be all together in Bombay but Baba will be close by. Here Ma is so far away. I had a lovely holiday. It was awesome. Apart from those few days when it rained non-stop. But even that was better than the rainy season in Bombay because there was no school and no university and Baba and I were together all the time. What I most enjoyed in those days was reading aloud to each other. Baba used to read aloud to me a lot when I was little. Easily the best part of the entire holiday was the caravan holiday! But before we leave there is a big event coming up. That is Baba's birthday. I want to buy him a book and have a big celebration. I have made a plan. That will be a wonderful end to the holiday.

7. *The English and Creative Writing Department*

'Shall we head to the pub up the road for a drink?'

Samrat ground out his cigarette beneath his heel with undue emphasis and looked at Caroline. 'I'd love to,' he said, swallowing the 'but' that was about to follow.

'So let's go.'

'I'd love to but I have to go home to make dinner for my son.'

The lecture on writing memoirs had been enjoyable. It had been a packed house and the writer who had been invited to deliver the talk had been witty, erudite and engaging. Caroline and he had been walking towards the railings to which bicycles were chained when she had asked. It was getting on to be 7 p.m. and the blue depths of the sky were flecked, like afterthoughts, with a few clouds. Arnab loved to look at those clouds and liken each of their shapes to a tree, an animal, a bird, some mythic beast even. There was nothing Samrat would have liked more at this moment than to walk up the road and have a drink with Caroline.

He would love to, but he really had to be home to make dinner for his son.

'I'd better be getting my bike, then. See you,' Caroline said as she walked towards the bicycles, not turning back to see Samrat wave at her.

Samrat was attached to the Department of Media Studies, but the department he really wanted to be a part of – knowing that he would never be a part of it – was the Department of English and Creative Writing. Samrat was a reader, a close and voracious reader. Like many readers, he believed that writing a book was like taking just one step forward from reading them. If only I had the time ... Samrat wrote advertising copy for a living – clever, funny advertising copy – but that was not real writing to him. Real writing was what several members of the Department of English and Creative Writing did; they were the ones who had their names on the covers of books; and they were the ones whom Samrat was – though he would never have admitted it – in awe of and envious of at the same time. He had never seen so many writers together.

Within days of arriving at the university, he had taken to spending time at the English and Creative Writing department. He had attended public lectures and seminars, introduced himself to the writers he had read and spent time with some of them in the staff bar. These are the guys with real swagger. If only I had the time.

Caroline Cusk was doing a PhD on the manipulation of time in the novels of Henry James. Samrat had met her at a lecture by a world-famous Irish author, who was a devotee of James. Samrat found James boring and convoluted (he had not actually gone beyond *The Aspen Papers*; he had not even got to the end of *The Aspen Papers*) but he had attended the talk because he was an admirer of the Irish writer.

Caroline wanted to be a writer. She knew that, unless she got lucky (and she was pragmatic enough to not count on it), she would need a day job. The PhD was a means to securing a teaching position, perhaps at this very university. She was working on a novel. She talked a lot about how hard it was to write, how insecurity and confidence warred with each other in her mind.

Samrat found it fascinating to listen to her talk about her struggles; he had never known anyone who talked about these things. The writer who had moved into Imperial Heights, the writer he admired, had never told him any of this. Like most readers, he could not imagine the arduousness writing demanded.

'I want it to be short: forty-five to fifty thousand words or so. Ian McEwan writes somewhere of that being the most perfect length for prose fiction. Long enough for the reader to inhabit the world of the book and short enough for her to finish it in a sitting or two.' Samrat shook his head in wonder; it seemed strange to him to have a novel defined by the number of words it comprised.

Caroline knew all about the mid list and agents and which publisher wanted what. All this, the whole process, the nuts and bolts and pulleys behind the finished object that was delivered into a reader's hands, the whole world of the writer and agent and publisher – when explained in the way that Caroline did, a world as quotidian as that of the carpenter or plumber – that world was a revelation to Samrat when he met Caroline.

Samrat was a visiting fellow at the university at which Caroline was a student. But when it came to such things, their statuses appeared to be reversed.

Once or twice a week, they would meet in the period between Samrat finishing his work at the university and returning home for lunch. Samrat enjoyed going to the students' bar with the huge TV and permanent aura of indolence. He loved sitting outside, loved the trestle tables and the sun high in the sky, the heavy deep ashtrays and faded beer mats, the way in which he had to hold on to his glass when it got really windy, the leaves swept up into whorls in the field alongside him. And all those perfectly shaped, scantily clad young bodies in the sun, among them Caroline's, all that *youthfulness*, their lives stretching out in front of them, the sense that they had all their mistakes yet to make and all their joys yet to look forward to. It did Samrat good to be in the proximity of so much hope. He liked this more than the staff bar with its stuffiness and self-importance, its air of faintly concealed plotting and softly aired grievances. There, he felt like an interloper.

But their brief meetings had about them a feeling of thwarted possibility. It was as though something was being denied the chance to begin. Samrat was always looking at his watch, attentive to being back home on time. And with Arnab at the 'Bates Motel', it seemed impossible to be able to meet anywhere else at some other time.

On one occasion, Caroline had said that she had tickets to a literary festival in Cheltenham. A Pakistani writer Samrat admired was giving a reading. But it would be a day trip (at least) and what would Arnab do? He was unlikely to enjoy the festival and he couldn't be left behind.

The thick tyres of Caroline's bicycle spat out bits of gravel. Samrat turned to walk back home. But he didn't right away. He sat on the rectangle of grass in front of the main library and lit a cigarette. In the distance, he could hear the thwacking of tennis balls, punctuated, once in a while, by a shout of outrage or self-castigation. It was a chilly day for late spring. What to cook for lunch? Would those two boys turn up to play football with Arnab this afternoon? And if they did, could he … No, it wasn't so much whether he could. *Would* he? He had come to England to spend eight weeks with his son. At no point had he thought that it would be anything but uncomplicated.

The smoke burned his throat. Samrat felt a double constriction: the manner in which his life had narrowed with the departure of his wife and son from the home that was theirs; and within that diminished life, a further narrowing at not being able to – in this town that he had never visited and would never again come to, in this extended spring, among relative strangers – pursue what he was sometimes tempted to.

The ash of his cigarette, grown long, keeled over on to the grass. The breeze blew specks of it into Samrat's eyes. He blinked rapidly, but could not get rid of them. Plump and watchful, a red squirrel examined him from the foot of an oak. Lunch, then. Bangers and mash.

8. Homogeneity

After the first six weeks, it rained. It wasn't the sharp burst or sometimes barely perceptible cleansing drizzle of spring. It didn't pour as much as it threatened to wipe things out.

First, the south of England was on a flood alert. And then, it got flooded. From the window of their flat it appeared to them that they were less in this cathedral and university town than amid the hostile relentlessness – and relentless hostility – of the Bombay monsoon.

It drizzled at first, of course – moisture hanging in the air, making acute the smell of the earth and grass and flowers, a dampness in the fast stiffening breeze – and then it really began to rain. The grey sky at the height of spring, the fields filling up like bogs. The squelchiness. The nuisance. The nothingness. The sky: nothing. The fields: nothing. The colours: nothing. The spring: nothing. The homogeneity of this English rain. It was the uniformity of the Bombay rain.

Where had it all gone, the light changing every so often, the clouds, as they tore or ambled across according to the dictates of the wind, now brushed with crimson, now with orange, now with purple? He looked out of the closed window, its smudged pane beaded by hurrying droplets that plopped and burst when a gust violently directed another wave of rain at them. How the torrent had swallowed all vividness.

Cooking. Cleaning. Caring for. Reading. Reading aloud. And always the rain. The curtain of it, intensely uneventful. It seemed as though even the rain was tired of falling but couldn't help itself, could do nothing to stop itself from going on.

On a day like one of these, Rakesh had come to the Chaudhuris' Bandra home to ask for a job.

9. 'I want to pay for your birthday cake too'

Ever since he learnt that he was coming to England with his father, Arnab had begun to save money. He had asked Malini to not buy him presents from money that relatives or parents of friends gave on special occasions. He stashed away his own pocket money in a faded denim purse that Samrat had once got as a freebie and passed on to him. Every week, his mother gave him a crisp twenty-rupee note. His father did the same. Arnab had discovered that one of the few perks of being an inhabitant of a broken home was that his pocket money had doubled; neither of his parents had the heart to stop giving him the money because the other was.

Two days before leaving, Arnab went to the bank with Malini and traded his savings for pristine currency in sterling pounds. He stared at the face of the Queen on the notes. 'She doesn't look at all like the photos I have seen of her!' he said, pointing to the notes.

How a world of opportunities had then opened up. Arnab bought all that he wanted: a spiral notebook from Tesco; second-hand books; a mug with a photograph of Windsor Castle; an inflatable ring that he intended to use in the pool when he returned to Bombay; football boots at a closing-down sale on the high street.

One of the reasons why it is hard to be a child is that you are penniless all the time and this experience – the act of dipping into his purse and being able to instantly gratify the desire for an object he fancied – seemed to Arnab to be a window into the many pleasures of being an adult.

But he spent well within his means. He knew that his father's birthday was coming up and he wanted to give Samrat a treat. 'A return gift for bringing me here,' he told Samrat as he outlined his plan for the day.

After a certain age, one's birthdays hold significance only as events that one's children enjoy celebrating. While Samrat delighted in Arnab's enthusiasm, he also tried to find ways in which the boy would not end up spending too much money on account of his birthday. He knew he shouldn't, not really, but he would feel guilty if Arnab splurged on him money he had so scrupulously saved up.

On Samrat's birthday, Arnab set the alarm on Samrat's phone and rose before his father. He made breakfast (cereal, cold milk, toast, blueberries, juice out of a carton) and arranged it all on a tray. The piece des resistance of the presentation was a single daffodil, picked the evening before, nodding in an empty bottle of Stella Artois that he had saved from being chucked in the bin.

All day, he took photographs. With the phone. With the iPad. Arnab belonged to a generation that needed photographic evidence of any and every occurrence for it to feel authentic. And he had no use for a camera.

For days, Samrat had been resisting Arnab's idea of buying him a book as a birthday present. In Waterstones, he winced when he saw the prices of titles he wanted. But the morning's paper had offered a solution to this impasse. In that day's edition was a book coupon. All you needed to do was to present the coupon at any Waterstones outlet. Then, for 99p, you would get a copy of Richard Ford's *Rock Springs*. The wonders of marketing literature creatively.

Book swinging in its bright red plastic carry bag from Samrat's right hand, they walked across to the cathedral precinct. In the blocks of shadows cast by the cathedral, the grass was cool. A flock of gulls, perfect in a diamond formation, streaked purposefully somewhere. Far above, a plane trailed vapour.

'Baba, I want to pay for your birthday cake too.'

'Cake? Where did that come from? I don't want any cake. You know I don't eat cake.'

'No, Baba, just for today. See, the book didn't cost as much as I thought it would. I saved money. I want to buy a cake for you.'

'But I don't like the sweet cakes at the Swan Bakery. *You* like them. Why don't I buy one for you?'

'You buy them for me all the time. Why can't I on your birthday?' Suddenly, Arnab pumped his fist and grinned. 'Yes! Idea. I won't buy you cake. I'll buy you cream tea. You love that, don't you?'

Samrat rubbed the small of his son's back. Arnab leaned in towards his father. Defeated (by logic) and triumphant (with happiness), Samrat smiled at Arnab and said: 'Let's go. You'll want an ice cream, I am sure.'

Of the two big bakeries in town, Samrat preferred the one near the cathedral. He liked its low ceilings, steep staircase and the garden at the back. If you sat here, the sound of traffic did not reach you and the susurration of the leaves was amplified.

Arnab preferred Swan Bakery on the high street. He liked their cupcakes, the Mr Whippy ice cream stall alongside it, sitting out at one of the tables and watching people on the street.

Each wanted to go to the other's favourite. Finally, a deal was made: Arnab got his way with paying; Samrat got his way with where they ought to go. So they turned up at the Swan, a group of teenaged girls parting to let them pass through the middle, Samrat clasping Arnab's hand inside his jacket pocket.

Arnab ordered at the counter and paid. The lady who brought the order to them said: 'What a polite boy you have got here. Never forgets to say "please" and "thank you". So soft-spoken. When I look at some of the others over here ...' She rolled her eyes.

When she had left, with the food displayed before them, Arnab played the happy birthday tune from a guitar app that he had downloaded on to the iPad.

Samrat ate slowly, cutting open the scone, hot and fresh, smearing the pieces with clotted cream and jam, not bothering to prod at the bits that got stuck between his teeth, not even, for once, brushing away crumbs that fell on the table. Arnab raced through his cupcake. Then he grew his chocolate moustache as the ice cream melted in the unseasonably warm day. All the while, he took pictures. Of the scones; the bakery; the man on the street in a ripped leather jacket and a purple mohawk; the young woman in a translucent summer dress, the sunlight passing through it and rendering visible the contours of her breasts. He took photographs of his father. Most of all, he took pictures of the two of them together.

That night, Arnab did not sleep in his room. He wanted to sleep with his father in the bed in the larger room. Arnab slept towards the wall. He turned towards his father. Samrat lay on his back: after having broken his ribs and been forced to lie only on his back for months, he had grown comfortable sleeping in a posture he had never before adopted in his life. The fingers of his left hand were entwined with those of his son's right.

When Samrat looked at all those photographs later – and he looked many times, with great absorption – he was most struck by one of him and Arnab. It came to exemplify for him that particular day, that particular holiday, that particular period of his life, and theirs together. The chairs were arranged side by side. They were leaning towards each other, anxious that they were both entirely in the frame. Their temples were touching. Crumbs stuck to Samrat's lips. The ice cream cone was in Arnab's tense grip. Slightly out of focus, behind them, was the back of someone who was leaving the bakery. Above them, a patch of sky, uneventful, unlike the past.

10. Yes

Malini said yes.

Two days after his birthday, the day before they were scheduled to board the plane back to Bombay, Samrat made the phone call. He had been thinking about this for months, but it had come to entirely occupy his mind since his birthday.

Sitting on one of the sofas in the faculty bar, he called her. The only other people present in the bar were two professors who were discussing a PowerPoint presentation on a laptop open in front of them.

Malini and Samrat spoke for a long time. Yes, she had been thinking, especially over the past two months. Yes, it had been very hard on Arnab; she often felt that their son was torn between them. Yes, they deserved another chance, all three of them. And so, yes, they would have a go at it again. Yes, they would talk at length once Samrat and Arnab returned to Bombay. And, yes, Malini and Arnab would move back in to Imperial Heights.

Samrat wanted to tell Arnab right away. At the same time, he wanted to be on his own for a little while. He sat down on a bench close to the path that skirted the football field.

That early afternoon in spring, on the eve of returning home, beneath the vastness of a cloudless sky, life seemed full only of wonderful possibilities.

A BIG DAY

On the morning of her annual piano concert, Tanvi woke up with a familiar sense of anxiety and excitement. She awoke gradually, maintaining her position of lying on her left side, her fist a pillow for her cheek, allowing her sleep-dulled mind to clear, holding on to the state of being awake, just about, but not alert.

The curtains were drawn, but in her room, facing east, there already was light. Tanvi squinted, hooding her eyes with her palms, looking at the patterns of light – blocks and stripes and serrated shapes – that fell on the doors of the wardrobe built into the wall opposite her bed. She glanced at the watch she wore even to bed, its once-pink strap now an indeterminate colour, but its radium glow still as invaluable in telling her the time in the middle of the night as it had been when her parents had given it to her, inside a velvet box bound with a pink ribbon, one

Christmas many years ago. A quarter to eight. It was going to be a big day.

Leaving her bed, she picked her way across the floor over the blanket that she had kicked off at night, a pair of slippers and a soft ball and, opening the door of her bedroom just a crack, peeped out. This was her ritual on a Saturday morning: to feel the pulse of the household before she yielded to the tug and flow of her own day.

There was the piano lesson in the morning, a final, frantic brushing up, repeating the drills on their own and together – coordination and harmony among the players as important as individual skill – before the concert in front of a packed auditorium in the evening. After the lesson, the day would stretch before her, as these days always did, long and yet not long enough, a slow wind up to the evening's event. She was the best in her piano class and scored the highest among her peers in all the Trinity School of Music examinations that she had taken, but her piano school – for reasons unknown to her or her parents – had dispensed with solo performances this year. Tanvi was, at the same time, glad that she wasn't playing on her own this year, without the acute loneliness of being up alone on that huge stage, dwarfed by the grand piano, and slightly resentful that, because she was playing as part of a group, the plaudits of a solo performance would be denied her.

The maid, Savita, on her haunches, was mopping the living room – the perfectly geometric arcs she left on the floor drying quickly under the swiftly spinning fan. There was a faint smell of cleaning liquid and disinfectant. Tanvi heard the electric kettle bubbling in the kitchen, the clang of a pan, the lid of a jar being set down on the counter and the water running in the sink – all the sounds heightened by the weekend morning quiet. She sensed her mother's presence in the kitchen.

In her parents' bedroom on the other side of the living room, the curtains were dark, extra-thick black fabric having been stitched on to their undersides so that not the feeblest glimmer of light penetrated the room irrespective of how late it was in the morning. There, Tanvi knew, her father was still asleep and would be till much later. She was pleased that he had again kept his promise: he was not travelling on work and would, as he did every year, attend the concert. When she came on to the stage to play, she always tried to pick out her parents in the crowd. That they were there was both a source of sustenance and trepidation; she wanted to revel in their pride of her and was wary of the slightest slip that might wound that pride.

Buttering a slice of toast for her daughter, Sunita Chandiramani tried to focus her mind on the big day that lay ahead. She had known when she had woken up that her mind was made up. She would confront her husband this morning. She had lived with the knowledge of his infidelity for months. She had decided that they would have to talk about it and that she would have to bring it up. When exactly she would call for this discussion was all she had been able to think about for the past few days. Now she knew that it would be this morning. It was hardly an ideal precursor to Tanvi's concert, but nothing could be done about it; there wouldn't be a better opportunity than today. Manish would be at home all day; because of the concert there was no party to go to in the evening; and she would get the time – more time than she was ever likely to get with Manish – in the morning when Tanvi went for her piano lessons as well as after their daughter had gone to bed.

This would be a day like no other. Too bad that it happened to be the day of the concert.

As she put out the breakfast things on the table, elements of the plan clicked into place. She'd give Manish no time to prepare himself. She'd simply tell him that they needed to talk and that this morning was the best chance they had. To pull this off, she'd have to do what she had never done before: let the driver take Tanvi to her piano lessons. Then they would be on their own at home.

Inside his pitch-dark bedroom, Manish Chandiramani stirred and stretched. He awoke with an indistinct sense of unease. He had been dreaming of the woman he had been with on his last business trip. It was disquieting, this dream, as though it were a double infidelity. When he threw open the curtains, the room turned radiant with sunlight, which swept across the lacquered floor as though keen to conquer it.

Outside, he could hear Tanvi practising the piano, a Schubert concerto, music he loved to listen to not merely because it was music he enjoyed, but because it was his daughter who was playing. He could imagine her sitting upright on the piano bench, the rigidity of her posture somehow a comment on how sacrosanct this activity was to her.

Manish showered and shaved quickly. A look at the bedside clock, its alarm muted today, told him that Tanvi and Sunita had already finished breakfast, and that if he wanted to see his daughter before she set off for her piano lesson, he had better hurry. This was a big day in his calendar, the annual concert in the evening and however much he had been away, to whatever extent he had missed watching his daughter grow up, this was the one event he had never failed to attend.

'You'll be there, won't you, Dad?' Tanvi had asked when the date of the concert had been announced.

'Yes, have I ever not been?' he had said, and here he was, happy that he had honoured that commitment to his child. As he dressed, he again puzzled over what it was about his wife that had been bothering him these past weeks. He felt a niggle about it, the anxiety made keener because he was unable to unearth its source.

Sunita sat down at the table as her daughter ate. 'I'm not going to drop you off to the piano school this morning,' she said. 'Sajjad will drive you. He'll wait there and then bring you back.'

Tanvi choked on her mouthful of toast. 'You are not going to come with me? You are not even coming to collect me?' Her eyes wide, she looked like a caricature of herself. 'Why suddenly?'

This was one of the matters about which mother and daughter had routine run-ins. Tanvi was the only one of her friends who was not allowed to travel unaccompanied with the driver. This elicited sniggers and put-downs in the school playground, at her piano lessons, on the basketball court. Tanvi fretted, chafing to unshackle herself ('Why can't Sajjad drive me on his own? Why do you have to *always* tag along? I am not *little* any longer'), but Sunita would brook no discussion on the subject. 'If I have told you once, I have told you a thousand times, Tanvi. I have explained. I don't want to discuss this.'

And now, over a mouthful of toast on the morning of her concert, there was this.

'Why suddenly?' Tanvi asked again, keen as much to satisfy her curiosity as to hold on to the sense of liberation her mother's decision had endowed her with.

'I have some important stuff to sort out at home.'

Unconvinced, Tanvi smirked and shrugged; never had any stuff been so important as to keep her mother from accompanying her.

'Listen, you take my mobile phone.' Sunita slid her phone across the table.

'It's only the piano class, Mom. I don't need this.' Tanvi jabbed at the screen with a marmalade-kissed index finger.

'Just keep it with you.'

'Can I play Pacman on it?'

'I thought you were going to play the piano,' Sunita said, in the way that was so familiar to Tanvi, withholding a yes while not explicitly saying no.

When Manish, in his track pants and white Ralph Lauren polo shirt, the fragrance of his shampoo and aftershave preceding him, emerged into the living room, Tanvi was hurriedly collecting her things, ready to leave. A child who usually had such exemplary composure, she made a frenetic spectacle of leaving the house, dropping things, gathering them again, forgetting something, running back into the bedroom for it, retying her laces or readjusting the strap of her sandals, her departure announced by clatters and stomps, cries of panic (from her) and remonstrance (from her mother).

Manish noted that Sunita was wearing a pair of capris and a faded T-shirt, her preferred stay-at-home set of clothes. When was she going to get changed? Weren't they getting late?

Despite his wayward schedule, intemperate drinking, unruly eating habits and the lack of an exercise regimen, Manish was still a good-looking man. His hair was thick, black with slivers of silver. He wasn't as trim as he once had been, but the erectness of his bearing and the careful choice of clothes made him look fitter than he really was. ('Not like that Samrat Chaudhuri,' Manish often said, referring to his neighbour. 'Just look at him. He has simply let himself go after his wife left him.') His skin had on the whole remained remarkably smooth and youthful, accentuating the faint laugh lines beneath his eyes.

One of the things that made him attractive was that he carried around with him, even when at his most relaxed and unassuming, the imprimatur of success, the aura of a man, impossible to mistake, who was rich and commanding, used to giving orders and having them unquestioningly obeyed. This bearing attached to it a certain kind of glamour that some found irresistible and some others tried to imitate but, not having acquired the authenticity of his success, fell short of.

Manish walked up to his daughter, who was on her knees, stuffing into her bag an exercise book that had tumbled to the floor. Manish bent down and kissed the top of his daughter's head. 'Practise hard. It will be great fun in the evening,' he said.

Tanvi spun around, a little too hard and, slightly losing her balance, ended up in a sitting position on the floor, her legs splayed out in front of her, her weight resting on her arms. 'Dad, I am going on my own. Sajjad is driving me.' Her raised inflection carried double exclamation marks at the end. 'And he will bring me back. Mom is not coming.'

Manish looked at his wife, who refused to meet his gaze. 'Hurry up, Tanvi, hurry up,' she said. 'Why must you make a mess of things like this? You'll get late. Get going, go on.' Tanvi, too delighted to let her mother's imprecations mar her mood, only smiled back. She knew she would not be late for her class.

'What's going on, Sunita?' Manish asked. 'Why aren't you going with her?'

'We need to talk.' She looked at him now.

Neither spoke. The silence between them was defiant and combative.

With a final, frantic flurry, Tanvi departed, waving her goodbyes. Sajjad was waiting downstairs in the car.

The heat, even at this hour, cannoned into them through the windows Tanvi had on purpose lowered. Precisely because her mother would have had the air conditioning on, Tanvi didn't this morning, revelling in the uniqueness of the occasion. The air conditioning, while more comfortable, insulated the car's passengers from their surroundings, the street cries and sense of lived life outside: the harsh croak of a gaggle of crows scavenging at a torn paper bag on a street corner; the stream of invective let loose by an auto driver as a bike cut into his path; the distant but omnipresent hammering at a construction site; the sound of the engines of all the vehicles around them, of various tones and pitches; the snatches of conversation, in front of shops just opening for business, from autos and bikes that travelled alongside their car – the bits of conversation being at the same time comprehensible on their own and meaningless because they were divorced from their contexts.

They went down the hill, past the fruit and vegetable market stalls with their bamboo and tarpaulin frames, where custard apples, pomegranates and sweet lime, in perfect architecture, were arranged like pyramids, where massed arrays of red onions lay on beds of jute and plastic packets of basil and thyme, galangal and lemon grass, caught the sun and glinted like minor treasures.

The piano school was on the third floor of a nine-storeyed building. A large apartment, its original layout now hard to imagine, had been converted into classrooms, practice rooms (or labs, as they were known), a reception area, and a toilet. Sajjad parked outside on the road and entered the building a pace behind Tanvi, who was skipping ahead, her bag swinging from her left shoulder in determined, uneven arcs. The lift had a collapsible door, made of diamond-shaped metal grilles, which, after it had been pulled open, rapidly slid shut of its own accord. The trick was to hold it open, keep it open by force, enter the lift and then allow it to close. The buttons on the panels were intransigent; they never worked till you had poked them a few times. As Sajjad entered the lift behind her, Tanvi raised herself on her toes, trying to see how much taller she needed to be in order to see the reflection of her face on the stained mirror on the wall.

When they walked into the apartment that was the piano school, there was no one around. Only the young man who mopped and cleaned sat behind the reception desk, sullen, glancing through a Marathi newspaper. He wet his index finger by licking its tip, and used it to turn the pages over, stopping now and then at the odd news item that caught his attention, reading it with frowning concentration before flicking the page over again.

Uncertain of what to do next, Sajjad stood in the doorway. Tanvi glanced at her watch, realizing that she was earlier than usual, earlier than anyone else, including her teachers. She waved to Sajjad. 'Wait downstairs, Sajjad Uncle. I'll be down once the class is over,' she said in a voice that had as much firmness as politeness and was an impersonation of her mother's. Sajjad nodded and turned away towards the lift.

Sunita would never have stood for that; her rule was to wait for one of the teachers to arrive.

Blinding white was the colour scheme inside the school – the walls, the blinds, the desks, the sofa in the reception, the cushions. On the far wall, to the left of the reception desk, was a small shelf (white) on which stood a six-inch-high marble figurine of Ganesha (white), rotund and beady-eyed. Two sticks of incense burnt at this altar created for him.

Glad for the air conditioning after the hot car ride, Tanvi sat down on the sofa facing the reception desk and, pulling her mother's phone out of her bag, began a game of Pacman. Kicking off her sandals, she bent one of her knees back on the sofa and, impatient and distracted, started to tap the cool floor with her other foot.

The young man – a boy really, a teenager, not much older than Tanvi – observed her as he did every time she turned up for her piano lessons. He observed the other girls too, but he always looked out for Tanvi.

He lived in that patchwork quilt of slums, very colourful squares and rectangles of tarpaulin of different hues one saw just before one's plane nosed down towards Bombay, the sweep of the sea stretching across this city by the ocean. Along with his mother and brothers, he had to queue for water from a communal tap from three in the morning.

This job that he had, cleaning and mopping the floors for these rich children, went a long way towards keeping their household of his consumptive father, mother and two siblings, alive. He didn't have a sister. His father's frail health would not have been able to stand that.

His mother was a maid. His father, once a construction worker who had come to Bombay from Bihar, could no longer earn any money. He had been sacked from his job because the tuberculosis no longer allowed him to carry those huge loads of bricks – carry them so far and for so long. He just coughed these days. And spat out blood. After that, he drank away a large part of the income his brothers, his mother and he brought home.

The boy was disciplined. He neither smoked nor drank nor sniffed glue, although all the friends he had in his slum (the teenagers, the young men, the wage earners, the ones in control of their families' destinies) were addicted to something or the other. One of them, who worked in a pharmacy, had a stash of bottles of expectorant that he purloined from the store; he consumed bottles and bottles of the stuff every day; he distributed his largesse as well.

Several of them stole and robbed. Some of them had been arrested, been taken to the police station and beaten. A few of the parents had been able to bribe the police officers at the station and get them off.

He was proud to be clean. Inside him burned an anger, incandescent, white hot.

Tanvi had had enough of Pacman. She put on her sandals and walked into one of the labs. None of the teachers had arrived yet. Tanvi glanced again at her watch with the faded wrist band.

He waited for the door to the lab to close, waited for her to be alone in that room with the grand piano, brown and burnished, shining, on the white white floor, against the white background. She would be sitting with her back to him and the music would muffle the sound of the door being opened.

He waited. It was still too early for anyone.

Then he made his move.

IF THERE WAS NO HOPE, WHAT WAS THERE?

Savita was so used to being beaten by her husband that she didn't mind it all that much. What was there to it? Only beating. God knows, men did worse to their wives. She only had to look around in the slum in which she lived. Men burned their wives with cigarettes. Threw acid on them. Locked them up without food and water. Why, three shanties down, one man had even killed his wife. Stabbed her six times with a kitchen knife and gone to jail.

He had not broken any of her bones. Nor had he disfigured her in any way. Savita was grateful for that. Narendra only had a temper. He was easy to anger. In those moments, he could not control himself. Of course the drink was partly to be blame for it. But that was not the sole reason. There was just something about his anger. Otherwise, he could be kind and caring. His job as a plumber paid well. He put food on their table. Only last month, he had bought a TV for them. Savita could now watch movies and Hindi soaps at home; she no longer needed to go to her next-door neighbour's. He was saving up. He said he wanted to move out of this rented place and into a home of their own.

But of course she minded being beaten. Their daughter was always there. She saw it. Savita minded that very much. Don't hit Ma, don't beat her. Narendra heard nothing when he was beating Savita. Anger insulated him from everything. He was focused.

Of course it hadn't always been like this. There was the memory of their courtship. Furtive meetings at distant street corners. Narendra leaning against a lamppost, his face yellowed in the frail light of the bulb above. A visit to the cinema not so much for the film but for the chance to be alone in the dark. Savita remembered only the title of the film they had been to: *Dhoom*. Their secret was inevitably outed. Clinging to each other, finding strength in each other amid the storm of reproach that broke from the families. Finally, the wedding and this room in Khar Danda, the sea a presence in their lives, freshly caught fish drying in wicker baskets not far from their door.

The beating had begun shortly after Asha's birth. They got worse after the second daughter, Lata, came. Lata lived with Narendra's parents in their village. It was less expensive that way. Asha, who was six and going to the local free school, was with them. The village was a four-hour train ride away. Savita saw Lata only when she went back to the village for a fortnight during the Ganpati festival. They couldn't afford the train fare too often. And she wouldn't be allowed so much leave anyway.

Daughters, fucking daughters, two of them. Fucking witch, couldn't bear a son. Head slammed against the wall. Did she do this on purpose? Stomach punched. Who will pay for their dowry? Will the dowry come from a bloody maid's salary? Bitch. Face smacked. Can't have a son, who would have fetched a good dowry, made things easier. Fucking cunt, sucking my blood. Leg kicked.

No, no bones were broken. She was not disfigured. That was a miracle.

When was the first occasion that Savita had been hit? She had put too much salt in the dal. Asha was eight months old then. Narendra had come home late. He was tired, bitter about something. He was worried. He had said not a word as he sat down on the floor to eat. Savita put his dinner in front of him. He tore off a piece of chapatti, dipped it in the dal, put it in his mouth and spat it out on to the floor. He flung the bowl across the room where it clattered against the opposite wall. Dal snaked its way downwards. Narendra got up. Savita was still sitting cross-legged on the floor. She did not see his hand coming. He had grabbed her hair and pulled her up. She still had not anticipated the blow. His right hand, still dribbling. Her left cheek.

On that first occasion, Savita had felt not so much pain as shock. My husband is beating me.

Fucking cunt. Can't even cook. Can't even give me a proper meal at the end of a hard day's work. Work that buys food for this brood.

She worked too. She worked hard all day at all those apartments at Imperial Heights. She made more money for her family than many women she knew. And she cooked and cleaned and kept house.

Only to be beaten?

He had pushed her. She had fallen over. By the time he had started kicking her, Savita had curled herself into a ball. The shock and the shame had been subsumed into pain.

There had only been the pain.

Afterwards there was always the fear. Week after peaceful week, but always the fear. The peace seemed like an interruption before another bout of violence. When would his mood change? When would he be violent again? Savita could barely enjoy the peace in the terror of waiting for the beating to start.

But she didn't mind that much. God knew, men did worse things to their wives. It wasn't as often as it sounded. And Narendra did care for her. He simply could not control his temper. And where would she be, with only her maid's salary? How would she get by with the children? It was unthinkable to go home to her parents. They would not stand for it. She would not allow herself to do it. She thought of the TV. She thought of the new home. She thought of the expensive sari he had bought her only this past Diwali.

Most of all, she thought of Asha – and the future they must give her. Asha would not be like her. Asha would go to college. Asha would find a proper job. She would be independent. She would never have to rely on a man. Asha would not need a dowry to get married. That was where Narendra was wrong. Their daughter would be different. Why would dowry ever come into her life? But what if it did? What if things did not turn out as she hoped? What then? This was the main fear that prowled Savita's mind. That it was too naïve to imagine such a future. That nothing would change. But she must hope. If there was no hope, what was there?

Savita was thirty-one years old. When she wore her chiffon sari during Diwali, kohled her eyes, put on her anklet and bangles, carefully painted a tiny bindi dead centre on her forehead, she could sense Narendra's eyes on the men on the road, checking to see if their eyes were on her.

Looking at her, you couldn't tell that she had two children. Two daughters. Big difference. Narendra had wanted them to have another go at it, to have a third child, a son this time for certain, how could their luck not turn? Savita had been terrified. What control did they have over such things? And what if … She had said no.

He could do anything, but no. She had held out. She had suggested, one night, that Narendra have a vasectomy just to make sure.

She remembered every little detail of the beating she had got after that. Her body was a map of unprecedented, unimagined pain.

Several of her employers thought that when she worked in their apartments she felt envious; they thought she resented their affluence. Some of them, but by no means all of them, made sure that their purses and wallets were never there when she entered their bedrooms or studies. Don't put temptation in the way of the weak. But they needn't have done that. Savita knew her place in the world. She hardly ever felt resentful of the wealthy inhabitants of Imperial Heights. She did not particularly pity herself for the hard scrabble life she had. It wasn't good or bad, hard or easy. This was just how it was.

She had her pride. She was proud of her job, proud of the fact that she was good at it, that she worked so hard at it, that the money she earned made a difference to their lives. She had her own aims and ambitions in life. Her world was a different one from that of her employers'; she knew it was never possible to cross over from one side to the other.

That sort of thing happened in Hindi films. Or did in real life if you became a successful gangster, a don, a real estate developer or got lucky or were blessed with extraordinary brains or good fortune. Savita knew she had been blessed with nothing out of the ordinary. And that, as far as she was concerned, was that.

Her work was always held in high regard. That she found pleasurable.

On her haunches, the bucket to her right, the mop making Shailesh Patil's marble floor shine as though painted with wax, she never let up till things were just so, till she saw her reflection on the floor gleam back at her just a touch brighter than when she had started mopping. Chopping potatoes at Priyanka Dandekar's, she ensured that no julienne was thinner or thicker than the other. Having scrubbed clean the kitchen counter at Samrat Chaudhuri's, she left the plates stacked in precisely the same order every afternoon, the smaller ones in front, the mugs left hanging every day from the nails fixed into the wall in the exact rectangular formation that Samrat liked. At Manish and Sunita Chandiramani's, she vacuumed the carpet and curtains with scrupulousness, not stopping till even the hint of a speck of dust had been sucked in, been done away with.

All this was appreciated. From every household, she received her Diwali bonuses on time; she got hand-me-down clothes from the Chandiramanis; often tokens of appreciation in the form of cash from Shailesh and Priyanka. Samrat passed on sweets or chocolates and, when ordering in pizza, almost always ordered an extra one for her to take home to Asha.

The apartments she went to spoke to her of the state of mind of their inhabitants, the state of their lives. Shailesh's was like a mausoleum. He had not thrown away any of Nandini's old things. He worked to keep the order and arrangements of furniture and lamps inside the flat just as they had been before. But because things were not the way they were before, the apartment was full of absence, of a silence that no amount of noise – even at the New Year's Eve party that Shailesh hosted – could drown.

One morning she had seen Shailesh talking on the computer with his son and daughter-in-law in America. It was wondrous, like a phone and a TV put together. Savita had crept up, and keeping her distance, she had stood from where she could watch and hear. The pictures so clear of their home over there, a house with many rooms; it seemed it was night there while it was morning in Bombay. It would have been nice had she been able to see Lata like that once in a while.

Now half the size her previous home, the knocked-down wall back up again, Priyanka's apartment was alive with a sense of contraction. At least that is not what had happened to her. Narendra was still there, life was much as it had been. Stasis, when she saw Priyanka, seemed like a good thing to her.

She was very fond of the boy, Sachin. His father's death had seemed to have endowed him with a new sense of poise and dignity. He was always reading something or the other. He was good at his school work. And when he watched football on TV, his eyes blazed with a fierce intensity. Savita often sat quite still in a corner of the living room and watched Sachin watch football. It calmed her to see such self-absorption. Savita remembered that the final week of the year used to be a time of great celebration in the Dandekar family. Ajit and Priyanka would both take that week off from work. There would be a huge party on Christmas Eve. The towering tree the Dandekars got every year would stand, strung out with fairy lights and tinsel and crackers, for a week in a corner of their massive living room. If all the other lights were switched off, its glow would be bright enough to illuminate the living room. There would be lots of gifts for Sachin at the foot of the tree, gifts he believed Santa had brought him. He was a small boy then. One year, he had asked Savita: 'What did Santa get your daughter?' 'Santa doesn't come to our home,' she had said.

Savita was convinced that her daughter would have to be good in English. Not just learn English after a fashion – as she would in her government school – but be really good at it. That was the key. And she had to be able to speak it well. Speak it as the people Savita worked for did. With fluency and confidence as though it came instinctively to her, as though it was the only language she was comfortable in.

Savita had bought from a pavement stall a book from which Asha could learn the alphabet. But merely that wouldn't do. Someone had to teach the girl. Someone who spoke the language as though it were his mother tongue. She would ask Sachin. That would be perfect. Priyanka was always kind to her; she would allow it.

Asha. How much hope she had invested in her little girl…

Samrat's home conveyed to her the sense of a life that had been interrupted. Like when you hit the pause button while playing a film on DVD. Savita knew she had been somewhat neglectful of her duties at Samrat's. There was no one to keep track of what she did (or didn't). She knew it wasn't fair, it pricked her conscience, but she was only human, wasn't she?

She missed Malini and Arnab. She missed seeing the three of them sit down for lunch together on Sundays. How did a woman find the strength to leave her husband? Was it money? Was it something else? What had made her do it? One thing had not changed from before: the empty bottles of expensive wine continued to stand in rows in the cupboard beneath the kitchen sink. Savita sold them to the raddiwala every Sunday morning. What did these people drink? Would Narendra behave any differently if he drank one of these things rather than the plonk he did? Was it what he drank? Or was it how he drank? No beating seemed to be going on in any of the households in which she worked. But beneath the surface, behind the closed doors, in the time that she wasn't there, things must go on of which she knew little.

Manish Chandiramani travelled abroad a lot for work. Hardly a fortnight went by in which he did not make a trip. His suitcase was always packed. Besides, the family went on a holiday overseas nearly every year. Their apartment was a shrine to the places they had been.

There were miniature bells from a host of countries on top of the sideboard. The doors of their fridge were covered with magnets. Savita read the names on the magnets – she could spell out the words in English, she was clever; had she been allowed to continue with school, she would have been good at her studies – she read the names, London, Florence, Paris and tried to relate those names to the photos she saw on the magnets: a bridge, a church, a tall tower. She wondered what those places were like. She had once watched with Tanvi, the Chandiramanis' daughter, a DVD of their family holiday halfway across the world somewhere. On seeing it, she had felt the jolt of the unfamiliar.

She had herself never been on a holiday, only once to Nashik for the day on a bus with twenty other people from the slum. It was dusty. There was a long queue at the temple. They had returned late at night and she had fallen asleep on the way back. It had been very tiring. She couldn't see what there was to enjoy in it. But if they were to be able to go to a beautiful place one day, just for a few days, wouldn't that be nice? She needn't open a bank account. Money doesn't grow on trees, Narendra kept saying, but money grows in a bank. She didn't even need a bank. If only she could set aside some money every month, in an old cardboard box that she could hide away, then perhaps in a year, maybe two years, they might be able to go on a holiday.

She hardly ever saw the Chandiramanis enjoy a meal together, hardly ever saw Manish and Sunita sit chatting with a drink or a coffee of an evening. Manish was asleep when Sunita left for school with Tanvi. Sunita taught at the university. By the time Manish returned from work, his wife and daughter had gone to bed. On the weekends, they always had people over or went over to someone's place. For a university professor, Sunita often appeared to her as absent-minded. Occasionally, she would be in a really foul mood. Savita knew that her employers had the right to her time, but she never forgot the occasion when Sunita had yelled at her, had threatened to sack her because she had not come to work one morning and had not let Sunita know.

Asha had been in bed with a raging fever that morning. Savita had had to take her to the doctor. It had been towards the end of the month and she had been unable to top up her mobile. There had been no way in which she could have called.

She scrubbed. She cleaned. She washed. She vacuumed. She chopped. She stacked. She made the beds.

She dreamt. She hoped. If there was no hope, what was there?

HAPPY NEW YEAR

The year his wife died, Shailesh Patil did not hold a New Year's Eve party in his apartment. But that was the only occasion when he hadn't. Even then he had thought for a long time about it, wondered whether the familiarity of the ritual would feel consoling or whether having the party without Nandini hosting it, being ever attentive to their guests, running the evening with her combination of precision and flair, would deepen his sense of loss. In the end, he had chosen to not have the party that year. All those people, all that talk – he could, at the time, hardly bring himself to cope with all of that.

But that had been the only instance; Shailesh's New Year's Eve party, with a single aberration, had returned to being as unchanging a fixture in the Imperial Heights calendar as it had been.

Contrary to the great Indian tradition of drinking on and on and finally sitting down to dinner when most of the guests were terribly drunk and in no state to relish the food on the table, Shailesh structured the evening in the style that is common abroad. It had been Nandini's idea, of course, and it had worked a treat. People started coming in from around seven-thirty in the evening. After a few drinks, dinner was served at nine. Once the food was over (and the generous amounts of wine with it), people went back to drinking. Most of them stayed back to usher in the new year at Shailesh's.

So there they all were: Manish and Sunita Chandiramani, Samrat and Malini Chaudhuri and Priyanka Dandekar – Shailesh's preferred fellow denizens from Imperial Heights. There were some who were missing from previous years, certain others who used to once live here and had moved out. Shailesh noted these absences. They spoke to him of something, he wasn't quite sure what. He refused to think too much; this was New Year's Eve.

Liveried men hired for the evening from a private agency had cleared and ferried away the dinner plates. Sated, some of them were still at the dining table, the food and the drink creating a pleasant torpor that made continuing to sit at the table a languid pleasure. Others had gravitated to the sofa, swirling and sniffing, sniffing and swirling replenished glasses of wine. They were tipsy enough to be voluble and loquacious without being so tipsy as to become abrasive and incoherent. Outside, there was already a steady stream of bangs and flares; from a little before midnight, tumultuous fireworks would erupt. That is when they would all gather around to watch from the balcony.

'Ah, well, that's another year gone. Should I feel nostalgic for it?'

'Depends on what sort of a year you've had, I suppose. I couldn't wait for it to be over.'

'But even assuming that you've had a bad year, how will its ending turn around your fortunes? The potency of 1 January is vastly overrated. It's just a date. It signifies nothing.'

'Well, it always seems like a new beginning to me. Renewal, rebirth, you know, that sort of thing.'

'To be born again, if you believe in being born again in the first place, you first need to die. I think Rushdie said something like that.'

'Well, it's a good time for gyms. You'll start seeing the ads from tomorrow's paper. Lose what you gained in the festive season. Discounts and deals.'

'I was reading somewhere that gym memberships go up forty per cent every January. And a small fraction of those who join – I can't now remember what that fraction was – actually stay on.'

'What a waste of money. Gymming is vastly overrated. Why can't you just run or walk?'

'Because you must do weights. Cross training. Only cardio is no good.'

'Why isn't only cardio any good? Why isn't only walking or running good enough in terms of exercise? It's just a capitalist trick, this whole obsession with gyms and the body. What's wrong with looking our age? Sculpted body, sculpted body ... Why not work hard at having a sculpted mind? And popular culture, TV, the movies, everything is feeding into this obsession with looking good, being thin.'

'Well, better a sculpted body than an unsculpted one, I say.'

'But that's because—'

'Stop, Samrat, please stop. Someone please stop him. I know he'll say the Woody Allen line next. "I don't pump iron, I pump irony." Someone please change the topic.'

'All right, Malini, I am going out to the balcony for a cigarette. Change the topic while I am away. I am not promising that I won't raise it again when I return. Now, where's my glass?'

'How inconvenient it must be to be a smoker these days.'

'Yes and when you watch foreign films made even in the 1980s, everyone was smoking.'

'People were smoking even on aeroplanes in the early 1990s.'

'Seen *Argo*?'

'Yes, superb.'

'But best picture?'

'At least no one else here tonight smokes. Otherwise, most of the party would have moved out to the balcony.'

'Very pleased that you could come, Manish.'

'Yes, Mr Patil, I remember I couldn't make it last year. I was travelling.'

'You don't travel much these days, do you?'

'No, very rarely. The odd trip to Bangalore. Perhaps once a month, once in six weeks.'

'His new job has been great for us. Manish has gone back to cooking. And he finds the time to teach Tanvi maths.'

'And watch films together. And listen to music. Yeah, off the treadmill. I am enjoying myself.'

'And how is Tanvi?'

'Oh, she is well. It took a long time for her to get back on track.'

'Ah, horrible, horrible business, that.'

'She is at home this evening with friends. We thought we'd let her be. We haven't come to a party together – the two of us – in a long time. And this is just taking the lift down. And it's New Year's Eve…'

'So has anyone changed the topic yet? Shall we talk about the elections? Or shall I start about gyms and our obsession with the body again? Wait, I'll refill my glass. Anyone else wants a drink?'

'I do.'

'Oh, what the hell, me, too.'

'Wait, I'll give you a hand.'

'Thanks, Manish.'

'When will you write a book, Samrat? You read so much. Surely, you have a book in you.'

'Ah, now don't get me started, Priyanka.'

'No, no, please go on. I am genuinely curious. As I am sure are the others. Mr Patil, don't you think Samrat should write a book?'

'He'd know best. Let's hear what Samrat has to say.'

'Well, I used to think that if only I had the time, I'd be able to write a book. I now know that that's all bullshit. Every writer is a reader, but not many readers are – or can be or should be – writers.'

'Why? What happened? How did you change your mind?'

'When I was away on that fellowship in England, you see, I met a lot of real writers. Proper ones, those who have published many books. Even ones who haven't yet, but surely will one day. And I saw that I was conning myself. I don't have what it takes to be a real writer. I love reading, yes. I truly admire many writers. But I am not one myself. And I'll never be.'

'Come on, you are being too modest. Besides, *everyone* is writing a book these days.'

'Yes, that's part of the fucking problem. Crap books, writers who are not readers, published, sorry, printed, by printers masquerading as publishers. These people are vain enough to want to be writers without even the least bit of talent or discipline. No wonder self-publishing is called vanity publishing. And then there is the web. You upload a fucking video or a song on the web and you are a filmmaker or singer. You write some drivel and go to Amazon and Amazon puts it out and you call it a book, you call yourself a writer. You are an *artist*. And let us not even talk about social media. People being self-congratulatory about what they are putting out on Facebook or Twitter. Soon, someone will have a bio that says: "He is the author of 50,000 tweets." It's all so terribly fraudulent. The frightening thing is that many people tend to take all this seriously. That is actually a comment on the state of our reading culture. I was reading a book by the British writer Howard Jacobson and he says something like: Soon we'll have no readers, only writers. That seemed so true to me, so true. Reading that, I made up my mind. Me, I'll fly the flag for the reader.'

'Well, never say never, Samrat.'

'No, well, phew, that was quite a speech, wasn't it? I need another drink. I want another cigarette.'

'I'll have one as well.'

'Go slow, won't you, Manish? Get the bottle away from him. Don't pour him that much.'

'Oh, come on, it's New Year's Eve. Happens only once.'

'What? It happens every year.'

'I meant only once every year.'

'But it's merely a date. Insignificant. Why don't we have a party on, say, the day of the winter equinox? There you go. Your drink. Ah, here's mine.'

'Oh, let's not go into that again. It's New Year's Eve. We are all happy. I love this day. I love this wine. I love the beginning of a new year. Cheers, everyone. Cheers!'

'That's quite enough love for now. Cheers!'

'How is Shankar, by the way? Are you in touch with him, Priyanka?'

'We meet once in a while, Sunita. He has been living in Borivali.'

'He didn't stay here for very long, did he? Not even a year.'

'Now, he is what I call a proper writer. Does he have a new book out soon?'

'I think I'd better go. My parents will soon be here to drop Sachin home.'

'No, no, don't go before the fireworks. Why don't you call your parents and ask them to come here with Sachin?'

'Err, I don't know, Malini.'

'Call them, call them. It will be good to meet Sachin. We don't see that much of him these days. How is he?'

'Oh, he's well, thank you. He's busy with so many things. He's got very good at football. That Chelsea Football School he attends has made a big difference. His grades in school have been fine. If only I could make him stop watching so much sport, they'd be better.'

'We should have a children's party next year. All the kids and all of us. Mr Patil needn't host it, for once.'

'Did I miss much while I was out smoking on the balcony?'

'We were just saying that next year we should have a party for all the children on New Year's Eve. I had run into Arnab and Malini at that new café in Juhu the other day. Arnab has grown so tall. I saw him after such a long time.'

'I have an announcement to make.'

'!'

'?'

'If we have a children's party, we'll have a new attendee.'

'What do you mean, Malini?'

'Just that I am expecting our second child.'

'Whoa. That's terrific.'

'Congratulations!'

'Now that is some announcement!'

'Lovely, lovely.'

'Malini, Samrat, I am truly delighted. Congratulations. A birth in this building after some years.'

'If I could bow without falling over, I would, Mr Patil.'

'Ah, there go the fireworks.'

'Come, quick, to the balcony.'

'Hurry, hurry.'

'Saw that one?'

'Fantastic.'

'How people think nothing of burning up all that money.'

'Oh, shut up, Samrat, it's beautiful.'

'Look! Look! Wish on that star!'

'You're drunk. That's a fucking Roman candle.'

'Hey, where's my drink?'

'There you go. Careful.'

'Oops.'

'Fucking hell. Now you have dropped your glass.'

'Get out of the way. Careful now. Who is walking barefoot?'

'Bloody hell.'

'Wait, I'll call one of these guys.'

'If only Savita were here.'

'The shards, the shards. Watch the shards.'

'Yeah. The shards are bastards.'

'Okay?'

'Yeah, fine.'

'Right. Okay. Now. Happy New Year, everyone.'

'Happy New Year.'

'Have a great one.'

'You too.'

'Happy New Year.'

'Happy New Year.'

'Happy New Year.'

ACKNOWLEDGEMENTS

My parents: Purabi Bhattacharjee (7 August 1947–23 July 2013) and Dilip Bhattacharjee.

Udayan Mitra, for getting this book spot on. And his promptness on email at all times.

Rashmi Gupta, Prema Govindan, Shatarupa Ghoshal and everyone else who, with immense forbearance, helped shape the journey of this book from a word file to a beautiful object.

Julian Barnes, friend, mentor, godfather of my daughter, for his enduring support and generosity.

Chandrani, my wife, without whom nothing is possible.

ABOUT THE AUTHOR

Soumya Bhattacharya is the author of five critically acclaimed works of fiction, non-fiction and memoir. His writing has appeared in the *New York Times*, *Guardian*, *Independent*, *Sydney Morning Herald*, *Granta*, and a host of other national and international publications. He has contributed to several anthologies published in India and abroad. He is the managing editor of *Hindustan Times* and lives in New Delhi.